Jack Connors and Sean Delaney, who've survived being hunted down by aliens, are living under assumed names in Mexico. They're finally getting over the events that sent them into hiding, but Jack is taunted by nightmares of his son, Nicky, calling out to him. Jack is traumatized as these episodes become more frequent, and he starts to worry that the secret government agency that was creating hybrid human-alien babies has found them.

Sean tries to calm Jack, assuring him that he is just being paranoid and fearful. But then nightmares begin to haunt both men, and strange things start to happen. Can everything they're experiencing be a coincidence? Are they hallucinating? Or are they about to find out that monsters are real and lurking just around the corner?

This book is a work of fiction. Names, characters, places, and incidents either are products of the author's imagination or are used fictitiously. Any resemblance to actual events or lo-cales or persons, living or dead, is entirely coincidental.

Nemesis
Copyright © 2018 A.J. Llewellyn and D.J. Manly
ISBN: 978-1-4874-2177-9
Cover art by Martine Jardin

Published by eXtasy Books Inc or
Devine Destinies, an imprint of eXtasy Books Inc

Look for us online at:
www.eXtasybooks.com or www.devinedestinies.com

NEMESIS
HAYWIRE BOOK 2

BY

A.J. LLEWELLYN AND D.J. MANLY

DEDICATION

To all those who believe something is out there.

It is.

"Just because you're paranoid doesn't mean they aren't after you."

— *Joseph Heller, Catch-22*

CHAPTER ONE

Jack stirred in bed. Something had awakened him. He grog- gily eyed the clock radio. Three forty-seven in the morning. The illuminated digital clock face disrupted his sleep all the time. Sometimes he covered it up, but Sean hated that. Had to be the former military man in him. He had to know what was going on all the time, each and every hour, even when he was sleeping.

This time, though, he couldn't blame the clock. It was the damned nightmares. The screaming echoes. Jack had to get up. His heart pounded, and sweat gripped him.

He's here . . .

Jack couldn't move without disturbing his lover, who slept wrapped around him. Sean was possessive, even in re- pose. Sean stirred and loosened his grip. Stealing his chance, Jack crawled out of the sheets. He slipped on shorts, his hands shaking. He felt vaguely stupid. They were home, na- ked and alone. No kids to worry about.

Or were there?

Calm down, idiot. There's nobody here but us.

Images from the past flashed in his mind. He tried to stop them as he walked out of the room. The dreams had been happening for weeks now. No. Not dreams. Disturbing, twisted night terrors. In them, his son, Nicky, cried out to him, begging for help.

"Daddy! Daddy!"

Jack moved quickly through the house. Nobody here. There was never anybody here, but he always checked. He took out the Glock he and Sean kept hidden inside a vase filled with Mexican paper flowers—a gift from the children of one of their neighbors. Gun cocked, he scanned the rooms he could see into, dreading the moment he encountered an intruder because he was certain that one day he would.

When you've experienced genuine monsters in your life, you never really live without them. And Jack had experienced some badass monsters.

He stopped and listened. The roosters that lived on the property he shared with Sean were quiet, but then they didn't usually start their ruckus until the first sign of daylight. He could hear the faint rustling of wind in the trees and, beyond it, the crash of surf. The sound still tickled him, a year after they had settled into their lives in rural Bajamar, Mexico. He loved Sean's rustic ranch, with its sprawling, faded white-walled house overrun by bougainvillea and grape vines. It still needed half its wind-broken windows replaced, and three-quarters of the roof had to be fixed, but he didn't care. Most of the time he felt safe here. And most of the time was better than nothing.

Best of all, they were only a mile inland from the Pacific Ocean.

Jack hesitated at the guest bedroom door. It was the one that secretly, in his heart of hearts, he would have designated as Nicky's room. He took a deep breath and opened the door. It was filled with little-boy things, for Sean had once been a dad, too. His son had been David. In a cruel twist of fate, Sean had adopted David from the same orphanage Jack and his late husband, Dexter, had adopted Nicky.

Of course, none of them could have known that David and Nicky were monsters. Hybrid, alien creations from some sick lunatic with plans to take over the world with mutant, perfect children. Each of the boys at Applegrove looked exactly the same, though none of the adoptive parents knew this.

They each thought they had wonderful, healthy, happy little kids.

Until their kill modes were activated.

Jack stood in the doorway and looked around. The father in him desperately missed his little boy. He pined for the small, loving child who needed him — Nicky, with his finicky eating habits and pathological fear of water.

Swallowing down the grief and panic he'd experienced in sleep, he sat on the bed, touching the antique Mexican bedspread Sean had bought for David long before he knew his own son was a scientific experiment sent to hurt him. Sean had suffered at the hands of the secret organization that was fast gaining control over the human population. Each time they watched TV and caught glimpses of little boys that looked like Nicky and David, they shuddered.

The children haunted both of them because when they looked again, the kids looked nothing like Nicky and David. Sean and Jack knew they were out there though. The people who made them were improving on their sample models. How many were there?

Some days, he could get through just fine. He could almost convince himself none of it had happened except that he was now quite afraid of the dark, and, frankly, so was Sean. They comforted one another. They felt safe in Mexico. Nobody had a call here for perfect, little white boys. They were all too busy coping with the kids they had.

Jack didn't want to think about little boys like David and Nicky being trafficked here as child sex slaves.

No.

It was bad enough having horrible dreams that his child was alive, held captive somewhere, being tortured, and screaming for his daddy. He'd seen TV shows of children held against their wills for years. In his worst moments, he had to work hard to remind himself this hadn't been Nicky's fate.

Something dreadful had lain dormant in Nicky. Some part of him had loved Jack, and he'd gone wrong in the execution of his order to kill. He'd finally turned into the homicidal alien he was supposed to be, but Jack liked to think that Nicky had resisted.

He focused on breathing. He imagined soothing Nicky from a nightmare and filling his head with beautiful thoughts. Sweet little Nicky, who would barter for vegan hotdogs and pancakes each and every morning.

"I miss you," he whispered to the empty room and began to cry.

Jack sometimes thought he was going crazy. Perhaps he was. Putting on a brave face as the transplanted Americano was, to him, like putting clean sheets on a broken bed. He was in pieces and didn't think he could ever be fixed.

Stop it. Stop it. You can't let Sean see you like this.

He rocked back and forth for a moment, trying to calm his nerves. He reminded himself that it had been worse for Sean. He'd been a fighter pilot and endured mind-numbing torture. Very occasionally, Sean would awaken in the middle of the night, screaming a mad sequence of numbers. He would shake and sweat but have no recollection of it in daylight.

Jack forced himself to relax. He would think about the ugly, homicidal alien creature lurking inside Nicky and cringe. His life had been turned upside down by the National Clandestine Service. He'd lost his husband, Dexter. His parents had been killed. He'd loved Dexter. They'd had a wonderful family life.

Stop that. It wasn't perfect. Sean loves you, and you have a fantastic sex life.

It was true.

He missed the old life not shadowed by fear. Okay, it hadn't been perfect, and there had been times Dex had driven him crazy not working, yet demeaning Jack's efforts to support their family.

Yes. Jack had lost everything. His cool studio job, his family, the life he thought he'd been leading.

He glanced at the door as he let his hand rub over the comforting knobs of imperfect, hand-spun silk in the bedspread. Sean was asleep. He sat and listened, but Nicky wasn't screaming for him anymore. Sometimes, his mind went back to that moment, when he and Dex took Nicky to Universal Studios in Hollywood for a long-promised holiday. He'd waited as Dex took Nicky for a ride, and still could not wrap his mind around the fact that by the time they came back, they were two different people.

Jack closed his eyes and took his hand away from the bed. In his worst moments, he wondered why nature, God, whoever, whatever, had punished him by tearing the life he'd created away from him. That moment when he'd seen a completely strange man and boy step off the ride and claim to be his husband and son was the second his whole life changed. Nothing would ever be the same.

He stood. Though the screaming in his mind had stopped, the love he'd felt for his son still clawed at him. God. He was crying again. He'd loved Nicky. He'd loved every minute of being his father. What did one do with all the love they had for their child, but the child no longer existed?

Jack knew first-hand the unimaginable pain parents who lost their children felt. It was unnatural to outlive your offspring. Even more unnatural to lose them to violence.

In Bajamar's coast-hugging golf resorts, he saw opulence. A few miles inland, where the real people lived, Jack saw street children, urchins, with hunger in their eyes, reaching to him whenever he and Sean made rare forays into town and shopped for necessities. They'd beg for money, and sometimes Sean and Jack gave them a few pesos, but mostly they gave them fish tacos from the famous Bajamar seafood truck, or, occasionally candy or ice cream. Money was taken immediately by the adults around these children who lived a merciless life. Jack would fret about them the whole way home.

He stole another glance at the bedroom door. Still no sign of Sean. He stood and took another lingering look at his surroundings. How wonderful it might have been to have a little boy here. To be planning their day. He imagined what he might promise Nicky. The thought made him smile. He would have promised fruit picking in the morning because they had an orchard filled with pears, peaches, and apples.

They'd maybe make a couple of pies, to accommodate Nicky's passion for carbs. Then he'd promise him lunch at the beach, at La Fonda, where they would listen to music and eat wonderful seafood.

He left the room and closed the door on such notions, even though his hungry heart bled for the child torn from him. He hurt so much he could practically smell the warm apple pies he imagined taking out of the oven.

Tears overcame him once more. He had to stop this. Had to get a grip on himself.

"Don't do this, babe."

Sean's voice behind him came as a shock, his lover's arms a welcome feeling.

"God." Sean took the gun from Jack's shaking hand and held him. He kissed his ear and suddenly said, "I dream of them, too."

Jack stiffened. They'd never spoken of them before. He pushed himself away, looking into Sean's troubled eyes.

"You . . . you do?" Jack couldn't believe it.

"I hear David calling my name." Sean blew out a breath and, with one arm still around Jack, touched the closed guest bedroom door with the other. He quickly retracted it, as though he'd scalded his palm.

Sean put the gun back with the brightly colored flowers. The tissue paper had held its brilliance even though the flowers were over a year old. The neighbor's kids had worked hard on the brilliant red, blue, green, and pink daisies, and the pretty yellow and orange tulip poppies that were considered a national treasure.

Jack watched Sean tenderly rearrange the flowers in his preferred style. They had everything in the house *just so.* That way they would know if somebody had been in here and done some snooping.

"Let's go back to bed." Sean kissed Jack's upturned face. Jack couldn't handle the idea of making love, though. He just wanted Sean to hold him.

"Or, how about I make you pancakes and coffee instead?" Sean asked, obviously sensing Jack's reticence. His rumbling voice went straight to Jack's cock. Yeah. Yummies first, then the *other* kind of yummies later.

"You shouldn't have mentioned food." Jack gave Sean a kiss he hoped conveyed the promise of pleasures in bed in their immediate future.

In the kitchen, Sean switched on lights. He'd bought the house, located a good two-and-a-half hours south of Tijuana, long before he met Jack. It had really been a wonderful find. Nestled in the middle of a ramshackle bit of orchard, the house had three bedrooms and two bathrooms, a living room with a fireplace, and a massive kitchen that they had recently discovered the previous owners had used to can and preserve fruit for market.

The interior of the house was pristine; a lot better than the outside would otherwise indicate. They hadn't wanted to draw attention to themselves as big-spending Americanos by painting the place and fixing everything up. Though officially called *gringos* by their closest neighbors, Jack and Sean weren't flashy types and never made much noise, literally or figuratively. After a recent, lengthy storm, they had helped one neighbor repair his roof, and the favor had been repaid, but Jack and Sean were not the social types.

Money wasn't a problem since Sean had hidden quite a bit in an underground safe in the warehouse in the backyard—the one-time canning and shipping headquarters. Sean bought the house under an assumed name, for which he had numerous pieces of ID and continued to use to update his F3 visa, to keep a bank account, and rent a mailbox at the post office in Rosarito Beach.

Besides which, Bajamar wasn't expensive. Sean was using three different aliases, all of which had ID, thanks to his former associates back on the mainland. Over time, Sean had built up a getaway plan, not thinking he would actually need it.

"Sean Campbell" was officially writing a mystery novel, and his friend "Jimmy Huntley"—Jack—was studying for a master's degree online, if anybody asked.

Neither was true, but they made for great covers.

There were only two drawbacks for both Sean and Jack. The first was the low-level anxiety of perhaps being followed. The fear sometimes flared to the surface that they'd be found by the alien-mongers they'd fled back in Los Angeles. It had been shocking how quickly the idea of a new Armageddon had died down after such a furor in California. In the year that had passed, it had been turned into a joke, the butt of every comedian on TV.

Even in Mexico.

But Jack and Sean worried. They knew the plans to produce other little boys, to send them off into the world to wreak havoc and mayhem, wasn't over.

They had no proof of this. Sean did a little online investigating but was careful to shield his ISP with firewalls and proxy addresses. The truth was out there, as the saying went, but he'd been unable to find it.

The other drawback was the sometimes stifling heat. There were public swimming pools all over the area, but neither man wanted to frequent them. There were way too many people, and the water never seemed clean.

That left the beach. Their house was far enough away from Tijuana that ocean pollution wasn't a problem, but they tended to head even farther south, to Rosarito Beach, where they blended in beautifully with all the vacationing *gringos*.

Occasionally, they would steal away for a day or two and drive down the coast. Baja California, as it was known, was simply breathtaking. Jack loved driving along the shores of the Sea of Cortez, looking for cool swimming and fishing spots, as well as tiny hole-in-the-wall cafes for lunch. The more time he spent with Sean, the deeper Jack fell in love with him. It had been like that from the moment they met.

As he sat at the kitchen table watching Sean rustle up their middle-of-the-night breakfast, Jack began to relax at last. The voices in his head no longer screamed, and he lamented his decision not to indulge in a little morning wood.

"Are you staring at my ass?" Sean suddenly asked.

Jack grinned. "You know I am."

"Well, you could have been enjoying it now, but oh no, somebody preferred to have breakfast." Sean turned and gave him a wink, then started flipping pancakes.

"I can enjoy it afterward, can't I?" Jack couldn't keep his gaze from his beloved's hot tush.

"Yes, Jack. You can have your cake and eat it. Get it? Pancake? Cake?" Sean wiggled his brows.

Jack couldn't help laughing. He jumped from his chair and went over to Sean, wrapping his arms around him from behind. Sean felt so good. Jack heard a noise and stiffened, but Sean kept cooking.

"Did you hear that?" Jack asked, his voice a whisper.

"Yes. An apple fell on the roof."

"No, it didn't."

Sean moved away from Jack and the stove and shot over to the back door. Before Jack could say a word, Sean had opened it and a second apple fell. The wind picked up, and a third apple dropped from the tree right next to the house. Jack bit his lip. He and Sean had hidden in the Angeles National Forest for a while, and it had been, frankly, scary. The desolation at night still haunted him.

And then came the moment Nicky arrived at their door. No. He had to stop thinking that way. It hadn't been Nicky, but a monster whose shell had been made to look like Nicky.

"See?" Sean kept a smile on his face. "Nothing to worry about. And we've got some extra bounty for breakfast."

Jack realized the pancakes were close to burning to a crisp. He was unable to move. He let Sean deal with them, and returned to his chair at the table. He missed his old life. He wished he could go back to being a normal man with a child. He hated hiding, feeling like half of him was missing.

Sean washed and chopped the apples and sautéed them in a pan. Jack's mouth began to water.

"Smells good," he said.

"I hope so." Sean threw him a smile over his shoulder. He opened the spice cupboard, and things sizzled on the stove as he added various spices to the pan.

Nicky and Dex had liked plain things. That's one thing I don't miss.

Stop it. Think in the moment.

Sean came to the table, juggling coffee cups and plates.

"Tell me about the dream," he said, forking a piece of apple and holding it to Jack's lips.

Jack was so shocked he took the apple with his teeth. Soft and buttery, it dripped with cinnamon and nutmeg. He chewed for a moment.

"Open," Sean said, forking a bit of pancake and feeding it to him. Once again Jack chewed.

"Better?" Sean asked, brushing back pieces of hair Jack didn't even realize were in his eyes. He blinked.

"Yeah, thanks."

Sean picked up his coffee cup and stared at him. "You've been having dreams for how long?"

The realization that Sean somehow knew and that it was okay to talk about it released so much tension in Jack he felt he would burst at the seams with relief.

"About three weeks."

"Me, too." Sean glanced away from him.

"How did you know I was having them?" Jack asked, picking up his coffee and sipping at it. Brilliant, as usual.

"You get all freaked out. I don't know if we are being . . . controlled somehow, if the idea has been planted in our minds . . . look, I know it sounds stupid."

"It's not stupid. I was there, Sean. I saw what happened. And besides, I've thought about it myself. Everything's been so lovely, so perfect."

"Yes, it has." Sean put the cup down and attacked his pancake. "We don't have any implants left. We checked for them." He chewed thoughtfully. "Maybe we've become so connected, we're sharing dreams now."

Jack gazed at him lovingly. "I've heard of that. Couples sharing dreams. I love you, Sean."

Sean dropped his fork onto his plate and groped for him. "I fucking love you, too, babe." With that, he picked up Jack, who kissed Sean's face the whole way back to their bedroom. Sean was already excited before they'd even begun to touch one another. Jack could feel his lover's need, and it was such a huge turn-on. Jack took hold of the gigantic cock that he still couldn't believe was his to enjoy. He'd fallen in love with it the moment he'd seen it.

"Why are you taking so long?" Sean asked, but he had a smile on his face as watched Jack playing with his favorite toy.

Jack stroked it a couple more times, then bent his head to the task of sucking. The crown was wide and thick and already slick, as Jack tasted the beads of moisture topping it. *Better than pancake syrup.* He licked and slurped at Sean's shaft, allowing it to ease into his mouth each time his tongue slid up from the base. He loved giving head, and Sean was a patient man who allowed Jack to take his time and savor each moment.

"I want you on top," Sean murmured.

"Somebody's getting impatient." Jack lifted his face for a moment and grinned at Sean.

"Not saying I want it immediately, but soon." Sean's eyes were glazed with lust. He propped another pillow under his head as he watched Jack suckle his cock. Sean moaned as Jack got back to work. Seconds later, Jack delved down to Sean's balls and ass. This was too much for Sean, who sat up and pulled Jack onto his face.

Jack shuddered as Sean began licking and sucking his ass. Jack steadied himself as Sean kept up a fast rhythm that had Jack ready to shoot in seconds. He lifted himself off Sean's face, but Sean stayed with him. Jack loved the primal sucking sounds his lover made.

"God, Sean, stick it in," Jack muttered. He felt as though Sean's entire face would enter him. The sensation was amazing. Balancing on his knees, he rose and fell, loving the way Sean kept up his aggressive sucking. Jack had no idea where their lube was.

Sean produced it suddenly from under one of the many pillows on their bed, but Jack was in too much of a hurry. His cock sprang upward. He slid down Sean's taut body until he felt his man's cock jutting forward. Sean gripped Jack's ass. Their gazes held as Jack worked his way onto Sean's cock. He couldn't believe how good it felt. A few seconds of pain and tightness gave way and Sean was inside him, moving deeper, harder, as Jack rode him in a slow, gyrating way. Sean grabbed Jack's cock, stroking him.

When Jack started to come, Sean cooed, "Come for me, babe." Jack wanted to wait for Sean but couldn't. His whole body caved in to the need as Sean began fucking him faster.

Jack came, Sean filling him with his hot seed seconds later. Jack didn't stop moving. He wanted to milk Sean's cock for everything he could get.

It was a fast and thirsty fuck. The perfect thing to obliterate night terrors.

Jack slowed to a stop atop Sean, who pulled Jack down closer. Jack hated when Sean slipped out of him but knew that he could have that wonderful cock any time he wanted it. He rolled beside Sean and said, "Lemme know when you catch your breath."

"My dirty boy." Sean kissed him.

"That's me."

"You know what I'd love to do today?" Sean asked. He lay beside Jack, grinning.

"What?" Jack touched Sean's hot face, enjoying the knowledge he'd made his man sweat so much.

"I thought maybe we could go to Rosarito Beach and have lunch at La Fonda."

Jack smiled. If that's what Sean wanted, he'd get it. He thought about how nice it would be to sit at an outdoor table, enjoy the best fish tacos on the Baja coast, and drink sublime margaritas and he immediately leapt out of bed.

"Let's shower!"

Sean pulled him back to bed. "Are you crazy? It's six o'clock in the morning. Get back in here!"

Jack laughed and let Sean pull him into his arms.

"Whatever you say," he told him.

Sean grunted. "That's better."

Taking their seats at their favorite seaside table at La Fonda Hotel's somewhat shabby restaurant a little after one o'clock, Jack loved the sounds of so many languages being spoken and different accents laughing. He particularly appreciated the two guitarists doing their best to drown out the just-arrived tourists, who kept griping about the appearance of the restaurant.

Try as they might, the musicians couldn't drown out the sound of the rhythmic, heavy surf.

Their waiter took their orders and returned quickly with chips, salsa, and two margaritas.

"*Gracias,*" Jack and Sean said in unison.

"*No es nada,*" the waiter responded. "It's nothing." He zoomed off again.

"I was thinking; we could go away for a week or two," Sean said, tapping some salt onto the back of his hand. He licked it, took a substantial sip of his margarita, swallowed, then sucked on a wedge of lime.

He winced only slightly. "Very good."

Jack twirled his drink, trying to decide if he wanted to lick, sip, suck, or just drink. He decided on the latter.

"Where were you thinking of going?"

"I don't know." Sean shrugged, glancing around them as he always did. He never sat with his back to a door or window when they were out in public. Clearly, he perceived everything to be okay because he repeated his salt routine. Smacking his lips with satisfaction, he let out a deep sigh. "That was tasty. Well, I was thinking some place in Sonora."

Sonora? Is he kidding? Jack said nothing for a moment. Going deeper into Mexico wasn't safe for Americans. They could be kidnapped and held for ransom. And since neither of them had anybody else in their lives, where would this leave them? They both knew this. On the other hand, he understood Sean was trying to come up with an idea that would get them away from their routine. Jack knew he'd been jumpy lately and this might help.

Getting kidnapped, however, would not.

"Where in Sonora were you thinking?" he asked, hoping he didn't sound tense.

"We loved that resort. What was it called?" Sean scrunched up his nose in apparent concentration. Yes, they had loved the Sea of Cortez resort, but Sonora was still notorious for its drug cartels and inexplicable violence. In the last six years, fifty thousand people had been murdered in Sonora at the hands of the cartels. Those were startling figures. Most recently, a Navy Vice Admiral had been ambushed and killed.

"The Sea of Cortez Beach Club," Jack said finally. They had flown there rather than driven since it was an eleven-hour schlep drive. They hadn't wanted to push their aged, but trusty, Lincoln Continental.

They had stolen it in California and driven it to Mexico. Since then, they'd invested a lot of money getting the car Mexican tags and keeping it roadworthy. Their mechanic, Manuel, had never indicated the vehicle shouldn't be driven distances. Sean and Jack had decided long ago it was better to be safe than sorry. The resort had been spectacular, and they'd loved the luxurious pool with its swim-up bar and the beautiful beach. The resort had been so lovely they hadn't even contemplated taking a drive anywhere. Yes, it might be fun to go back there.

He recalled the carefree feeling of shopping for fresh fish near the hotel and cooking in their room. They hadn't worried about being followed. The truth was, most of the time they'd been in Mexico they hadn't.

Up until now.

"That sounds like a great idea," he said, but when he glanced back at Sean, his lover had fallen asleep in his chair.

Jack shook him awake. "Am I that boring sweetie?"

"*666882. 666882. 666882!*" Sean shrieked, hitting Jack's arm away with surprising force.

"Oh, Jack. I'm sorry." Sean shook his head, his face pale and shiny.

Jack stared at him. When Sean first took Dex's place, claiming to be him, this was the sequence of numbers he kept shouting in his sleep. These episodes were usually followed by blinding headaches.

Sean seemed to be forcing himself to calm down. He stared at Jack in mute terror. "I didn't mean to hit your arm like that. I swear."

"I know you didn't." Jack reached a hand out to Sean, who took it. Sean hadn't had these episodes for a long time. He shook now, and Jack began to freak out when Sean let go of his hand and clutched his head. He hadn't done this in well over a year.

"Are you okay?" Jack asked feeling stupid and ineffectual. A couple of people glanced at them but looked away again when Jack made eye contact with them.

"I'm fine." Sean dropped his hands and leaned back in his chair. "That was weird." He gazed at Jack. "We'll talk about it later."

The waiter returned with a huge platter of fish tacos. "More margaritas?" he asked.

"Yes, please." Sean seemed revived now, but Jack knew that until they were alone, he wouldn't say another word about what had just happened.

Jack picked up one of the tacos from the sizzling metallic platter set into a weathered wooden tray. He longed to have one of those for his kitchen.

He opened the taco, stuffing it with guacamole from the platter, wrapped it again and bit into the soft, fragrant parcel. He nearly swooned. Better than he remembered. The cilantro and fresh tomato nicely set off the fish that he could tell was very fresh.

"Good, isn't it?" Sean asked.

"Very." Jack picked up his drink and took a slug. "Do you have a headache, sweetie?" he asked, sotto voce.

"No." Sean shook his head. "Weirdest thing. Later, babe."

Jack nodded. He liked knowing his lover wasn't in agony. That was something. They mowed through the tacos, enjoyed their second margarita each, then went for a walk and swim at the beach. A lot of men were fishing from the side of the wharf as Jack and Sean wandered the pristine white sand.

"Hey," Sean said, indicating the fishermen. "We coulda saved some money and caught our own lunch!"

Jack laughed. They never seriously fished. They liked to dangle lines and talk. Jack marveled at the fact that he and Sean never ran out of things to say.

"How do you feel about staying here tonight?" Sean asked.

"Sounds good." The hotel was a bit faded, but Jack liked the idea of not returning home. Yet.

They stayed in the water until the sky started to darken.

"Nobody says we can't eat at the restaurant twice in one day," Sean said as they walked back to the hotel, "and I'm jonesing for more tacos."

Jack grabbed his hand. "Me, too."

At the reception desk, they checked in and were pleased to find they'd been given a large room with a double bed positioned so that the occupants could look straight out onto the balcony and, beyond it, the sweeping sea.

The room was clean and cozy, furnished in a traditional way with Mexican blankets and de Grazia paintings on the walls. A fireplace gave the room an even more homey feel. Some small animal's head with tiny antlers had been mounted on the wall above the bed, however. Sean removed it and stuck it in the closet, knowing that Jack hated dead animals being used for decor.

They walked outside, admiring the chairs, tables, and thatched umbrella on their balcony. A colorful cascade of geraniums spilled from pots. Their gentle scent still filled the air, even though the sun was beginning to set.

Jack and Sean stood arm in arm, watching the ocean's thrilling show. Jack's spirits were lighter than they had been in weeks. The hotel's ambiance had an other-worldly feeling to it. Jack would have loved to hold onto the sensation. Room service, a bath together and sleeping with the waves soothing them to rest would be wonderful.

"I like it. Even the bathroom's great," Sean said. "How do you feel about room service?"

Jack laughed, looking up at him. "I was just thinking the same thing. I'd love it."

"Well, then." Sean looked pleased and took Jack by the hand, leading him back inside. "Come and test out the bed with me, babe."

Jack dutifully lay beside him, worried, because Sean seemed sweaty and nervous.

"Are you okay?" Jack asked.

Sean nodded. "Please don't worry." He reached out a hand, rubbing Jack's arm. "I was a little tense at first. But I'm okay."

"When was the last time you had one of these dreams?" Jack asked.

Sean blew out a breath. "Three weeks ago."

"And you said nothing?"

"You've had dreams too and failed to mention it." Sean leaned in for a kiss. "How about a little siesta, then we can eat?"

"Your wish is my command." Jack had hardly let out the words when Sean fell asleep, his hand still on Jack's arm.

Jack listened to the waves and felt Sean's breath on his face. He was afraid to close his eyes in case something happened to Sean.

I'm right here, he assured himself and surrendered his body to sleep.

For two nights, they stayed at the hotel—eating, drinking, sleeping, snorkeling. They felt good and rested, neither man experiencing any kind of nightmares.

"I think we should move," Sean said when they awoke on their third day in Rosarito Beach. "We can find a good place to rent. I think we should just look for something today."

"Where?" Jack asked. He loved their house, but the truth was, he felt better away from it. For now.

"Right here. We could rent a condo. I've been thinking we could talk to a real estate person. Tons of them around here. We could even rent a vacation cottage for a month or so."

Jack sat up in bed. "I love that idea! You really think we could?"

"Sure? Why not?" Sean swung his legs over the side of the bed. "Let's check out. We can have breakfast somewhere on the road and hit a couple of real estate offices."

Jack scrambled to join his lover in the shower.

Thirty minutes later, they'd visited one office only to learn they catered to honeymooners looking to plan entire 'destination weddings.' The woman behind the desk, however, was very helpful. She suggested they check out two different websites on which homeowners listed their own homes for vacation rentals.

The second office only wanted to deal with Jack and Sean if they wanted to buy and promised to make their purchase problem free. He rubbed three fingers together in the universal gesture implying 'for a fee.'

"Geez," Sean muttered, as they got back inside the car after their third such real estate office visit. "Even Mexico prefers to do business without having to actually deal with a real, live person. How many websites do we have to visit?"

"Eleven," Jack said. Maybe the website idea was better after all.

They drove home, still excited about their plans, and by the time they arrived in Bajamar, they were starving.

"You feel like tacos from the fish stand?" Sean asked as they noticed it was surrounded by a bunch of kids.

"Yeah, I do. We skipped breakfast!"

Sean parked, and they sauntered over to the food truck. A few of the kids recognized the Americanos and grabbed Sean's and Jack's hands.

Jack laughed until he saw a man in a ten-gallon hat bending over a little girl. He was talking to her in a soothing voice. Jack almost fell over when he saw her face.

She looked exactly like Nicky.

CHAPTER TWO

Sean and Jack left the food truck without buying a thing. Seeing the weird Texan guy and his kid had been very upsetting, to say the least. In the safety of their car, Sean took a photo of the man and his kid. He hated to admit it, but that little girl was the spitting image of Nicky. And David. Jesus H Christ! What if she was another one of those mutant kids?

The shock of seeing her soured Sean's and Jack's good moods and sent them scurrying for cover.

"Maybe we're over-reacting," Sean said several times before they even got home. Sean had a bad feeling about this little girl. What the hell was she doing down here in Bajamar? He parked the car inside the garage, then locked the front gate and the garage door. Not that it would do much good if somebody wanted to come onto the property, but the intruder would make enough noise to give Sean and Jack time to arm themselves.

Sean noticed only a couple of roosters as he and Jack went inside. Though wild roamers, Sean and Jack always left feed for the birds, but there were definitely fewer lately. Maybe the neighbors were eating them. Sean didn't want to mention it to Jack. He was stressed enough now as it was.

Inside the house, it felt warm and unaired. They opened a few windows and began walking through the house. It appeared that nothing had been touched.

Jack made grilled cheese sandwiches and cracked open a couple of beers, as Sean began working on the computer at the kitchen table. Sean watched Jack for a moment.

God, I love this man, and I don't want anything to happen to him.

Sean frowned at his cell phone, forcing himself to concentrate. By the time Jack joined him, Sean had loaded up the photo of the man and the little girl to his handy-dandy smart phone app that accepted an image, then surfed the Internet looking for a similar one online.

Jack gave him a kiss, as Sean hooked the phone up to the computer to see the results.

Bingo.

"Well, it says he's from Houston, Texas. His name is Lawson Marshall. And get this." Sean glanced at Jack, pausing. "He's a U.S. Marshal."

Jack almost laughed. "Marshal Marshall?"

"I know, right?"

"What's he doing in Mexico?"

Sean shrugged. "I can't find out too much, but it looks like he's been working on a few big cases in Texas. He might be here in the U.S. Marshals' Field Office."

"They have one in Mexico?"

"They've opened some in a few countries." Sean clicked on some links. "They pursue wanted felons from the U.S. who've fled, seeking refuge in foreign countries. The old way of doing business here is over. The Mexicans are honoring extraditions to the United States."

"Holy shit. What does it say about his family?"

"Nothing." Sean looked at him. "It's the same guy. I see him listed with the U.S. Marshals."

Sean studied Marshall's face. Tall, stocky and weathered-looking, he was the quintessential U.S. Marshal type.

"Maybe he's on vacation," Jack said. "Don't forget, we've got three golf resorts here."

"That's true." It didn't sit right with Sean though. He read through Marshal Marshall's brief biography. "Says he's done a couple of high profile fugitive apprehension cases." He read through another online report. "He single-handedly captured a fugitive who escaped from custody on the first day of trial for the gang raping of an eleven-year-old girl."

"Wow." Jack sipped his beer. "That's not a guy we want on the streets. Eleven? Geez."

Sean nodded. "And there's no proof he's working down here." His eye caught something, and he stared at the screen.

"What?" Jack sounded anxious. He had a right to be. When Sean remained silent, Jack repeated the question.

"The U.S. Marshal field offices are located in three countries: Mexico City, Mexico; Kingston, Jamaica; and Santo Domingo, Dominican Republic."

Jack grew quiet.

"I know," Sean said. "Mexico City's more than a day's drive from here."

"What if they're on vacation and all of this is a big, stinky coincidence?" Jack asked.

"Could be. We can only hope."

Jack toyed with his sandwich. "Yeah. And wait."

"Yes, babe. We wait. We may run into them again." Sean brightened at the idea of finding a new beach pad. "Should we look for the rental now?"

Jack, too, seemed excited by the idea. "Let's!" He moved his chair so he was sitting beside Sean. They ran through the online ads, narrowing their options down to two places. They gave up on the idea of Rosarito Beach, deciding they needed to get out of the area altogether. They looked farther south.

San Ignacio looked great. It was slightly inland but seemed charming and idyllic. In spite of seeing a couple of gorgeous houses online, they were wary of booking anything via Internet. Sean changed their ISP address, paranoid that their computer was being tapped. He did this constantly and had so far felt secure. He wasn't worried about his cell phone since nobody had the number except for Jack. They had nearly identical numbers and changed them frequently.

"We could just drive," Jack said. "Cataviña is supposed to be amazing, like another planet with all its desert and weird rock formations. It's only seventy-six miles from here. We could make a start today."

"Let's do it." Sean kept looking at the computer. "We can work our way down to San Ignacio. That's a couple hundred miles away. Lots of places in between. Just past Ensenada is that place we keep meaning to go to. You know, La Bufadora."

"Right. That geyser that reaches high up the cliffs every few minutes or so." Jack seemed to like the idea. Sean decided to leave the computer in the house. He took the gun out of the vase, however, and they packed up the place, tossing things they thought they'd need into a couple of small suitcases. Everything they owned they'd bought over time at yard sales—or Sean had brought them here before he and Jack came to stay.

Outside, however, disaster struck. The car wouldn't start.

Sean couldn't believe it. The Lincoln had been no problem at all. He and Jack exchanged incredulous looks. He opened the hood and was pretty certain the engine was inexplicably shot.

They took everything back inside. Sean pondered their problem. They were friendly with their mechanic. Sean called the guy, blocking his number.

Manuel arrived twenty minutes later in his tow truck. He knew Sean as Sean Campbell and Jack as his friend Jim Huntley. He stuck his head under the hood and tinkered around for a bit before announcing that the engine had seized.

"Time for new car," he said, smiling around a mouthful of gold. That's where Sean's cash had gone.

"How much to fix?" Sean asked.

Manuel shook his head. "New car."

They began to talk in Spanish. Manuel wasn't trying to make more money out of Sean and Jack. He had no car for sale and didn't know of any. He insisted Sean's car was no good and that replacing the engine was more money than the vehicle was worth.

Manuel offered to look for a car for them at a huge sale in Ensenada coming up in a couple of weeks. He said he had a friend who rented out vehicles by the week in Rosarito Beach.

"I can take you there," he offered.

"That would be great." Sean worked hard to sound grateful. Inside the house, Sean and Jack agreed they would rent a car for now, but they couldn't go with the guy with all their bags packed. Manuel would have questions.

No. They'd rent a car and figure out perhaps privately buying a car. In the meantime, they'd drive off on their trip in a couple of days.

"We can't act desperate like we can't wait to get out of here," Sean said. "Come on, babe. We'll be fine." Actually, though, he wasn't so sure himself. He was convinced the Lincoln had been tampered with, but he had no proof. He and Jack climbed into the cabin of the tow truck and endured Manuel's sometimes difficult to understand Spanish for the short journey to the rental agency. The signs bore the standard American Thrifty Rental Car company name, the place looked dilapidated, but the cars appeared to be in excellent condition.

Sean was shocked to see Marshall with a woman and the Nicky-faced little girl getting into a red SUV. Marshall had a set of golf clubs he was sticking into the cargo hold.

Marshall nodded at Sean and Jack as they waved Manuel good-bye and walked into the rental office.

"Afternoon," Marshall drawled.

"Afternoon," Sean responded. He could feel Jack shaking beside him.

The guy at the counter rented them a standard Ford Fusion and, after quite a bit of discussion, 'Sean Anderson,' who was on vacation here from Santa Barbara, California, had a rental car for a week. The rental agent discussed how they would handle Sean's desire to extend the lease. He became a lot friendlier when Sean purchased extra insurance for the vehicle, assuring Sean he wouldn't need to get a visa if he traveled along the coast for a few days.

"Only if you stay longer," he said, giving Sean his paperwork and the key to the car. Once inside the vehicle, Sean had to admit it was much nicer driving a brand new car than the tank that was the Lincoln. This car had everything, and he enjoyed touching all the buttons and gadgets on the dash.

"Look," he said, "Babe, we can dock our iPod here!"

Not that they had one. They had no electronics apart from the computer and their phones.

"The radio works," Jack said, equally excited. He changed channels, but it all frankly sounded the same to them.

Suddenly Sean heard *"666882. 666882. 666882!"* and stiffened.

"Did you hear that?"

"What?" Jack asked, looking tense again.

"Numbers." Shit. They were being followed and monitored now. Sean was certain of it. He suspected the vehicle had a tracking device, which meant they could not drive it on their getaway.

Easy, easy. You can go over every inch of the car and check it for bugs later.

"Since we had a rough day and the car's so nice, how about we have a nice dinner out?" Sean asked.

"Where?" Jack seemed so eager, but his eyes still held the anxious look Sean never wanted to see on his face again.

"How about Splash?" Sean knew it was a place Jack secretly yearned to try. Considered the best restaurant in Rosarito Beach, they'd never been, simply because it was the 'in' place and always crowded. On the other hand, if Marshal Marshall was here to spy on them, being in a big, busy place was what they needed.

"Are you serious?" Jack seemed incredulous.

"Very serious. Let's go."

"What about the marshal?"

"We'll see if he shows up."

Jack nodded. "Okay." He slid his hand onto Sean's thigh.

More than anything, Sean wanted to keep Jack safe. He didn't want to act squirrely and do something foolish and take off in case they were being watched. On the other hand, leaving the house in the middle of the night with their possessions — without the car — would be a great idea, too. They could travel by bus. They could find a car and purchase one. They could return the rental car in a week.

Sean's thoughts spiraled. He couldn't think straight. He was still wigging out over hearing the numbers over the radio, but since Jack hadn't heard them, maybe he'd imagined it.

He drove to Splash, keeping his eyes open for the red SUV, but it wasn't anywhere in sight. Jack was like a little kid when they pulled into the ritzy parking lot. *Wow.* Splash was as decadent-looking as it appeared to be on the odd occasion they drove past the seafood restaurant.

It was easy to see how it got its name. Huge rocks outside the back of the restaurant featured a water display. Jack and Sean chose an outdoor table and ordered margaritas as they perused the menu.

"Howdy," said a voice. Sean almost passed out. He looked up to see Marshal Marshall, the woman, and the kid.

"Hi," Sean said. Jack echoed the greeting.

"We saw you at the car rental place," Marshall said. "You're Americans, right?"

Sean nodded. "You are, too."

"We're from Texas. I'm here to play golf. The missus is here to spa."

"Spar?" Jack asked, looking shocked.

The four adults laughed. Mrs. Marshall finally spoke. "No, spa. As in facials." She smiled down at her little girl. "Julie and I had pedicures today. Didn't we, sweetie?"

"They used sugar for the scrub!" the little girl said. Her voice sounded nothing like David's, but her every facial expression was so like his little boy's that Sean couldn't take it.

He looked away, his head beginning to pound like a drum. Suddenly the little girl looked right at him. She smiled, and her words penetrated his brain like a sharp knife, even though her mouth never moved. *You can run, but you can't hide, Sean. David sends his love.*

He made a lunge for her, knocking the table over. Glasses fell to the floor, shattering, and the little girl let out a blood-curdling scream. Jack was trying to desperately claw him back.

"Let me go! Let me go!" Sean screamed. "It's not real . . . she's not a little girl . . . she's not . . ."

Something hit him hard in the chest, the impact throwing him back and onto his knees. He heard Jack shouting at someone, then everything got really blurry. The world was turning around him, and that girl, her face morphing into David, kept on smiling at him.

Oblivion was a relief, but it was short-lived. When Sean opened his eyes, he was huddled into the corner of a jail cell. *Oh no. This can't be happening. I can't be here. I have to get out of here.* There was nothing but silence around him.

He swallowed. "Jack," he whispered. *Where is Jack?*

Fear. It was the kind of fear that tells you that you're all alone and no matter how convincingly you say it or who you tell, no one . . . absolutely no one . . . is ever going to believe you. There was a scream at the back of his throat that never rose to the surface. He rubbed his chest. It felt sore. He'd been stunned or something. Didn't matter. They were here, and now he knew they were all around him.

He went to sleep again for a little while. He dreamed of numbers dancing in his head as he flew around the skies. *Captain . . . top secret mission . . . remember numbers . . . numbers . . . 666882 . . . all dead . . . all of them . . . dead . . .*

The door rattled, opened, and Sean's eyes flew open. Two men stood there, one in a white coat.

"Mr. Campbell," the white-coated man said, stepping forward. "May I call you Sean?"

Sean jumped to his feet, his heart pounding.

The lab coat came closer, his eyes a soft grey, a shock of white hair like snow cascading almost to his shoulder. "Now, don't be afraid, Sean, we're trying to help you."

Sean's gaze flew to the syringe in the man's hand. The other man, younger, with narrow dark eyes, wore the uniform of the Mexican police.

"You tried to attack a child, Sean," the doctor said, his voice meant to be soothing.

"Don't come near me with that. Stay away from me!"

"Why did you attack the child, Señor Campbell?" The police officer demanded. "She is very frightened."

"She's not a . . . a child. She's . . . well . . . she's . . ."

The police officer reached out and grabbed him. He seemed unusually strong, and Sean fought but to no avail. The needle sank into his flesh, stinging, final, and Sean told his mind not to let go of the changing face of that child.

He fell. He was falling and falling . . . as he walked through the aisle of the plane now flying on autopilot. *Dead.* All his unit dead. He turned and saw it, clear as day, not human . . . with blood red eyes and dripping fangs. A long tongue licked its lips as if it had just had a satisfying meal. "What do you want with me? What do you want?"

No answer was forthcoming as the plane spiraled down, suddenly out of control. Face down in the sand, then suddenly he was turning around in the air, going up and down and . . . he was at Universal Studios on a ride. He saw a boy sitting beside him, his boy? No. *Yes. Yes. He's your boy, Sean . . . and he shall show you the way.*

Little children, they shall lead us. Little Children . . . they shall . . .

When he opened his eyes, he was outside. The breeze was blowing through fragrant trees, and there ahead was a ship on the water just drifting . . . a port . . . harbor . . . San Francisco Bay . . . New York? No, Los Angeles, Hong Kong or . . . South Africa . . . Durban?

Aliens don't strike everywhere in equal measure. The first reliable assessment of the risk posed by ballast water has identified twenty hotspots . . . ballast water . . . yes . . . the seawater a ship takes in to keep it stable before it sets sail . . . um . . . makes us particularly vulnerable to being invaded by species stowed away inside the bowels of cargo ships.

It can't be.

At any one time, an estimated seven-billion tons of ballast water are crossing our oceans – this seawater is floating the seeds, spores, eggs, larvae, bacteria, and plankton native to wherever the water was loaded. The top cause of alien invasions worldwide is by ship, where they hide and thrive.

No . . . you don't expect me to believe . . . I mean . . . if you know this . . . why haven't you done something?

Not enough nations are willing to sign the treaty that would force these nations to dump this water before coming to shore. They can only survive in ballast water . . . warm . . . once in the ocean . . . cold water . . . whatever evil is there . . . dies.

Global warming.

Exactly.

We suspect enough have survived the journeys. They can take on any form they choose. Eventually, they will infiltrate and completely destroy us.

Why?

There was no answer forthcoming. Only the image of a ship fading in the sinking sun seemed to mock him. Sean sank to his knees. *Captain. Your mission . . . you must hit the ship from the air on its journey from Shanghai to San Francisco . . . you must drain them into the cold water before they hit shore.*

"You don't want this mission, do you?"

"No."

"Can you tell me what it is?"

"No."

"Then tell me one thing. Will you be coming back?"

Sean turned and looked into a face he'd once loved. *Laurence?* His lip trembled, and he swallowed. "It's not you. You're not real. Leave me. Leave me alone. Get away from me."

"Daddy, don't go."

Laurence stood there looking at him. He was holding David's hand. *My God. What is real?*

"My own men didn't rebel against me. They were dead when I turned around in that plane. Weren't they?"

Laurence nodded slowly.

"You took their bodies. You made them into . . . monsters." Sean took a step back.

"We're not monsters, lover. We're you're family." Laurence smiled the sweetest smile, and David looked up at him.

"We tried to save you, Daddy." David shook his head. "You just won't listen. You've been disobedient."

Sean turned and began to run.

"There's nowhere to go, Sean. We have taken over the airwaves and the military. Heads of state are falling, one by one. Soon, it will be over. Go with it, Sean. There is no pain."

Sean was running on the spot, and in the distance, he saw that ship. He ran harder, and soon the ocean rose up to meet him. He scrambled into the water and, as he did, the voices stopped. His teeth started to chatter together. *God, I'm so cold.*

It was an illusion. He was sure he was lying in some lab somewhere. They were ready to take his soul. He floated there on the water. He could see Laurence and David on the shore, looking at him.

"Jack. Where are you, Jack? Please don't hurt him."

Darkness surrounded him, and he was no longer sure if he was alive or dead. He sank into the icy water and felt the water fill his lungs.

It was over, or at least it had felt over until he opened his eyes and squinted into some bright, fluorescent lights. It took a while for his eyes to adjust. He was in a steel cage, no larger than four by six. His head scraped the top as he struggled to his feet. He looked around. Cages filled with ... people, and next to him someone familiar. "Marshall?"

The large man lay slumped forward on the floor.

"Marshall?" Sean hissed, not wanting to call attention to himself.

The man's head lifted, and he peered at him. "I know you."

Sean put a finger to his lips, shook his head. There didn't seem to be any of them around, but he knew they were close by.

The man inclined his head.

Sean kept his voice at a whisper. "What happened to you?"

"My wife and daughter they ..." He shook his head.

Sean nodded. "I know. They're everywhere. Did you see Jack?"

"No. They hauled you off. He followed, said he was going to try and spring you. That's all I know."

"Damn," Sean breathed. "We gotta get outta here, man. They'll erase our memories, implant devices . . . we'll end up their slaves."

"Who in the hell are these people?"

"They're not people. They're from elsewhere . . . don't know where . . . another planet or time . . . they plant seeds or spawn in the warm water ships take in . . . then they come ashore and they . . . well . . . they can look and seem like your best friend."

"What do . . . they want?"

"Total control and destruction of our race," Sean told him.

"Jesus. What happened to my wife and daughter?" He looked stricken. Sean couldn't do it any other way except to tell him the truth.

"They're probably gone, man. I'm sorry."

He knew the man wanted to cry, but he wasn't going to because anger had replaced his sadness. "Who are you?" He pressed his face between the bars and stared at Sean. "Why should I trust you?"

"I'm Air Force Captain Sean Delaney."

"No, Delaney mysteriously disappeared over Area 51, vanished during a routine mission at Edwards Air Force Base."

"Yes," Sean replied. "Area 51."

The man gasped. "You're a war hero. You fought two Desert Storm campaigns . . . trained by the Royal Air Force in Britain. Didn't you receive your stripes as Wing Commander . . . then you became a Squadron Captain in the U.S.?"

Sean nodded. "You trust me now?"

"But . . . why . . . how can you be walking around?"

"They didn't kill me. They tried to make me do their bid-ding, but . . . I held onto my memories . . . they haunted me. Wouldn't let go. Even now I'm not sure I know everything, but here's what I do know. They laid some sort of spawn or seed in warm seawater at various ports. This spawn must contain their DNA, and when they reach land, they multiply and invade us . . . like a virus. They don't seem to have a tangible form, at least not one they can sustain on Earth. They need our bodies, but our minds . . . our memories . . . are completely useless to them."

"It's already too late."

"No. It's not too late. I refuse to believe that. If they can only thrive in warm, stagnant water, then there are places on this Earth right now . . . shores they haven't reached due to geography. High mountainous regions for example. We need to get somewhere they haven't touched, warn these people, and get them to help us fight them. We can't trust anyone here anymore." As Sean said it, his heart sank. He knew it to be true. They may well have gotten to Jack already.

"Okay, let's say I buy your plan. First, we got to get outta here, then we got to get to some place they haven't been able to invade. How? By now I'm sure they've taken over the airports."

Sean nodded. "I know that, but I'm Air Force, remember? Flying us out of here won't be a problem."

The man smiled. "How do we get out?"

"Just follow my lead. They'll probably take us together. They don't know if I still have the implants or not."

"Implants?" His eyes widened.

"Whatever you do, don't swallow anything they give you. Oh, and ask for water."

He blinked.

"Don't worry, I'll tell you what to do with it when it's

time."

They waited. There was nothing else to do. The Marshall told Sean how he began to suspect something was wrong with his wife and child. It sounded like a broken record. He was worried about Jack. Had they gotten to him? Was he here? Had he escaped? Even if he was willing to take the risk, how was he going to find him?"

A slender man with a hawk-like nose came toward them. He smiled, clipboard in hand. God, they were champions at imitating human gestures and movements. "Good evening, gentlemen. My name is Roger Montrose. I hope you haven't been too inconvenienced." He reached over and opened Sean's cage. "We are so happy to have you home."

Sean smiled silently.

Roger Montrose opened Marshall's cage. "Please," he said, "come with me."

Sean glanced over to see two guards standing nearby. He met Marshal Marshall's eyes and knew the man had already taken note. The guards followed as they were led down a narrow corridor that smelled strangely like salt water. The hallway opened up into another room with stainless steel tables and strong florescent lights.

"Can I have a glass of water, please?" Sean asked the man.

"Of course." He smiled, motioning to another man, who stood nearby. The man scurried off. Sean glanced at the marshal, who was looking straight ahead. Sean tried to get him to look at him. *Ask for the Goddamned water!*

The man returned, handed Sean the glass. He, too, wore a white lab coat. Sean lifted the glass to his mouth, then caught the Marshal's strange look. *Oh, my God. Marshal Marshall is one of them!* Sean jerked the glass away from his face and tossed some of the water at Montrose, then the rest at the marshal. They both screeched like two wounded animals. Sean turned and ran through the open door down the narrow corridor. An alarm began to peal loudly, sounding halfway between a foghorn and a school bell.

He raced around the corner and up a flight of stairs, knowing they couldn't be far behind. On the top floor, he stopped short, his jaw slacking as he saw a door marked, "Incubation. Do not disturb."

Sean reached over and pulled hard on the knob. It wouldn't budge. He glanced down the hallway and saw an exit door. He ran to the end, hearing heavy footsteps pounding up the steps. It was a fire door. Sean yanked it open and scurried up onto the roof. He slammed the door shut, looking for something to bar it. He found a big piece of wood, but it wouldn't fit through the handles. There was nothing else.

Sean ran to the center of the roof just as the door burst open. There were Montrose, the two guards and the marshal, all poised to take him. He glanced down through a skylight, into a room below, where he saw rows and rows of test tubes filled with . . . something . . . murky white and water. The damn room was three-inches deep in water.

Sean looked up as Montrose came forward.

"Give it up now, Sean," he said. "It's enough. You know there's nowhere to go."

Sean kept his gaze on the skylight, feeling the wood still in his hands. "Where is Jack?" he demanded, breathing hard.

"Don't be concerned, Sean," the marshal said. "You don't need him anymore."

Sean looked up and lifted the wood over his head. "Sea water . . . warm . . . that's their embryonic fluid, isn't it?"

For the first time, the two men looked concerned. "Don't do anything rash, Sean," the marshal said. "Come away from there."

Sean knew he had one chance to get off this roof alive.

"You're going to let me out of here, or I'm going to smash that glass and destroy what's in those test tubes."

Silence.

"Make your choice!" Sean hollered.

Montrose lifted a hand. "Let him go." Smiling at Sean, he added, "We'll catch up to you soon enough."

Sean raced by them, taking the stairs two at a time. He ran until his lungs began to breathe in fresh air—until he could run no more. Reaching a street, Sean broke into and hot-wired the first car he found. He had to find a plane . . . oh God . . . and he had to find Jack. If they'd gotten to him . . . if they were going to use Jack to get to him . . . well then so be it. They'd either make it together or he'd die. Either way, Sean decided as he roared off down the street, he couldn't live without Jack.

Now, where in the hell was he?

CHAPTER THREE

Jack opened his eyes, disoriented at first, the words *Where am I?* on his lips until he looked around the dimly lit room and swallowed. His throat burned. His eyes hurt to keep them open. Turning his head slightly caused ripples of pain to shoot down the sides of his neck. He heard the plaintive whimper of an animal, then realized it was coming from him.

It's not possible. It can't be.

He was back in the hospital room where he'd been taken after his hysteria on the ride at Universal Studios.

"It's all right. You've had a very bad dream. You're going to be okay now, darling."

He turned his head just a little to get a closer look at her. Her gentle tone, the reassuring words felt like coming home. Her small hand on his arm comforted him. The effort of moving at all agonized him.

Jack could hardly speak. "Mom?"

She smiled. My God. It *was* her. The crooked bottom teeth. She was wearing the exact same outfit she'd been wearing when he first saw her in the hospital. They'd told him it was his imagination—that Nicky and Dex were not different people.

"Mom?" His heart almost broke repeating the word. He thought he'd never say it again.

"I'm here." She kept stroking at his arm, petting him lovingly. "You gave us all a shock," she said.

"How long have I been asleep?"

"You've been in a coma. We had to induce it. You injured yourself, and the doctors said you needed rest."

"Nicky and Dex . . ."

"They're fine. They're waiting to see you. You do want to see them, don't you?"

Jack stared at her. Could it be possible? Had it all been a dream? He couldn't think straight. He closed his eyes.

"Jack?" She raised her voice and tried to infiltrate his thoughts. He wanted his mother to be alive. He wanted both his parents to be here with him. But he wanted Sean. Not Dex. He began to feel guilty now for ever having missed his old life being Nicky's father.

"Where's Dad?" he asked, fighting to keep his thoughts clear. His voice came out in a rasp. Every letter he spoke ripped through him like a slashing knife.

"He's outside, too." Her face looked uncertain for one split second. "They're only letting us in one at a time."

"How long did I sleep?"

"The doctor will tell you."

"Mom?" He held her gaze. He had to keep it together, had to keep strong.

"Yes, darling?" Stroke, stroke. Her touch felt so good.

"I need water. Please. Please, can you let me have a sip?"

"I don't . . . I don't think we have any."

"Yellow water jug. Table behind you."

She gave him a dazzling smile and reached for the jug, pouring a little into a plastic cup. Her hand shook a bit.

"It's heavy." She'd noticed him watching her. She put the jug back on the table and held the cup to his lips. He batted the cup away, though the gargantuan effort to do so was excruciating.

He screamed from the pain.

She shimmered as water went everywhere. She began to roar as the water hit her face.

"My eyes! My eyes!" The alien creature posing as his mother dropped all pretenses and slithered back into its original, disgusting form.

Jack threw himself off the bed and onto the floor, scuttling under cover of the bed's metal frame. He wore only a thin hospital gown that was no protection from anything, let alone antagonized space lizards.

The alien had a tail and was spitting mad over the water. Jack rolled from one side to the next, avoiding the lashing, scaled tail that kept whipping at him.

Each move to defend himself hurt, but he had to fight. He had to fight hard. He caught a glimpse in his mind's eye of the torture they'd inflicted on him, and knew he had to keep moving, had to get away. And then something dragged him out from under the bed.

"Noooooooo!" He couldn't face more torture. Couldn't handle more pain. They'd shoved rods down his throat and into his ass. Everything had been designed to make him obey. Acquiesce. Give in. He twisted around and bit one of the hands holding his right leg.

A human hand, but an alien face. The alien screamed. Why the hell hadn't they just killed him?

The name Nemesis hovered in his brain.

"*Nemesis*," nameless, faceless voices whispered. "*Nemesis*."

Who the hell was Nemesis?

A pair of hands lifted him from the floor. Long arms. No. He shook his head. The Greys. Bad aliens. They'd been the ones to torture him, and they wouldn't stop. They didn't want him to die. They wanted to render him insane, helpless. Because everybody knew that people who were mad, who were deemed crazy, often had a stronger grasp of the truth.

But who would believe a madman who spoke of alien

children taking over the world?

Jack kicked the second pair of hands that grabbed him. He had to hurry. The metal clamps would come next. He couldn't live through another 'treatment.'

And that was when he realized it was payback.

Payback for destroying Nicky. For delaying their pet project.

"Fuck you!" he yelled, kicking, biting, scratching at the hands that held him. He realized he was being held aloft, about to be shackled once more onto the bed. The soft bedding fell away, and the cold steel gleamed up at him. A scream died in his throat when he saw the streaks of blood on it.

His blood.

Jack fought with everything he had. There were many of them. Six that he could see, but they hadn't expected a full resistance, and although one of them held a giant rod that could inflict brutal electricity through a man, he couldn't get it near Jack. The alien's large, oval eyes glistened with menace. This was a being who enjoyed inflicting pain.

Let's see how he liked a kick in the head. Jack thrust his foot into the alien's head. It felt gooey, making the creature rear back. Jack hit the metal table hard, kicking and punching at everything that moved. He grabbed the rod lying at the end of the bed. It was covered in blood and something else.

Feces.

The bastards. He thrust it at the two aliens still trying to restrain him. They backed away, petrified.

Yeah. Like all bullies, they loved to dish it out but couldn't take it in return. He held onto the rod, running from the torture room. He threw open the door and, in a long, dark hallway, saw numerous people of all ages and color waiting. Waiting. For what? Their turn for unwarranted punishment. They all wore hospital gowns and seemed in zombie-like states.

Abductees. That's what they were. Taken in sleep to keep them docile. There were so many of them. Jack couldn't believe it. Back on Earth—what the hell was he thinking? They *were* on Earth—people made fun of so-called abductees.

And here they were, proof positive of an alien race with bad intentions. The abductees all sat there like sheep.

He saw a little girl, however, who looked terrified. She caught his gaze.

"Run," he told her. Run!" She just stared at him. "You're in bed asleep. Tomorrow you'll think this was a nightmare."

She kept staring at him.

He got frustrated. He had no time, He had to run, but he couldn't let her be tortured. It would ruin her life. He snatched her hand just as the sound of dozens of feet began streaming out of the torture room.

"Wake up!" he screamed as he dragged the little girl along the corridor with him. Heads turned. The zombies were aware of him now. The little girl struggled to keep up with him. He sensed her total terror and so, he stopped, bending down to talk to her.

"I have to go, sweetie." He couldn't keep the panic out of his voice. "Tell your body to wake up. To let your spirit back in."

She did the staring thing again. "Tell your parents not to let you sleep in your room alone anymore."

That seemed to snap her out of it. The little girl must have woken up back in her bedroom because she suddenly vanished.

He took off running, and a quick look over his shoulder showed that a few abductees had followed him. That was no good. He had nowhere to lead them. Some began to vanish as their human bodies back in their beds awoke.

Jack ran through the dark maze of hallways. The sound of running feet close behind him accompanied him down endless hallways. He could hear voices yelling, accusing one another.

"You let him go!"

"No, *you* let him go!"

Still more voices. "Nemesis. We must find Nemesis!"

Who the hell is Nemesis? Do they mean me?

He ran from one corridor to another. A series of doors began to appear on either side of him. Glinting gold handles seemed to beckon him.

No way.

He took another turn. Heard the sound of a child sobbing.

Nicky.

No.

It was a little girl.

Jack could hear footsteps close. He was exhausted now, dripping with sweat. Yes, it was probably a trick, but his body screamed out in pain. He put his hand to the knob and began to turn.

No. Stop. You've come this far. You can't give in.

Never surrender.

The footsteps came closer, and he quickly turned around, opening a different door. The feeling of icy coldness enveloped him.

He had one chance, and he had to take it. He plunged himself into the room, closing the door behind him.

The crazy hell of the endless hallway seemed like nothing compared to the sea of ice in front of him. The place was dark, and his teeth began to ache. Every old injury he had flared to the surface. He couldn't move. And he couldn't see. Something huge and menacing hung close. Hands clasped him in the dank space.

Jack almost screamed except the hands were small.

"It's all right, mister. Don't be afraid," a small boy said.

Jack almost wept at the familiar voice.

Nicky!

"Son?" His hands groped wildly, his heart shattering for the child he'd been forced to lose. He fell apart right there in the cold, empty space of an unknown room. Hearing his son's voice was the worst kind of torture the aliens could have dreamed up.

Little hands kept tugging at him, and he surged forward, his bare feet slipping on a slab of ice. He grappled for purchase, on anything . . . something . . . but he began to slide down a thick shaft of ice, landing on what looked like an iceberg.

When he lifted his head, it didn't hurt so much. The frozen water had numbed his pains. He tried to get up, his eyes having adjusted to the peculiar purple-black light.

"I tried to help you, mister." The little boy who sounded like Nicky looked like Nicky, but wasn't Jack's son, landed beside him. Jack kept blinking. Around him, adults and children were climbing into ice boats. One woman held a black and white dog that panted heavily in her arms. Its fur was covered with ice, and each pant released thick curls of condensation. Huge men covered in strange pelts pushed one canoe after another into melting darkness.

"Where am I?" Jack asked the child beside him.

"It's the river boat launch pad, of course." The little boy looked at him as if he were crazy. "Come on. We gotta get in. It'll be a tight fit, but we can't leave you here, dressed like this."

"Where are we going?"

"To safety, of course. Oh, my! Are you nekkid under that thing you're wearing?" The kid waved his hand up and down Jack's body.

"Yeah. I guess I am."

The kid covered his mouth and giggled.

An adult handed Jack a thick fur and slung it across his

shoulders. "You'll die otherwise." What the hell kind of animal had Jack's fur previously been? Jack stared at the black and white dog that kept trying to keep its eyes open. A big, burly guy tried to take the dog out of the woman's arms, but she screamed and burst into tears.

"He's still alive! You can't take him. You've taken everything else."

The guy stomped away empty-handed and joined another guy at the rear of the canoe, pushing it out across the ice. Three sets of children in the middle of the craft began hitting the ice with their oars.

After a few hits, the canoe and the oars seemed to make a dent in the ice. The children paddled harder, faster, moving the vessel forward into inky, black water.

There was a dreamlike quality to all of this. It reminded him of *The Pirates of the Caribbean*, Nicky's favorite ride at Disneyland. There was no folksy music or any laughter here, though. Only a sense of grim desperation. He stuffed his hands in the pockets of the coat and noticed the long line of people in the distance.

Sheep! The thought triggered a memory, and Jack gasped. Holy cow! Sean had warned him about this.

He tapped the little boy who'd helped him on the shoulder. "Where are we going?"

"Wherever they'll let us land." The kid gave him that odd look again, as though Jack were crazy. "We travel this way because the aliens are afraid of water," the kid whispered, giving Jack a confident nod. "I have bad dreams about them sometimes. Do you?"

"Kid, you got no idea."

"Bad, huh?" The child slipped his hand into Jack's. Jack choked on the emotions that shot through him.

What the hell was going on here? Jack appreciated the warmth of the coat around his shoulders. He discovered sleeves and put his arms through them as he stepped into the canoe. The little boy had been right, but Jack didn't care that it was cramped. He wanted to get away from the aliens. How had he stumbled onto the right door and wound up in the right place so . . . so . . .

Easily?

He swallowed, watching other canoes slide across the ice floes to the occupants' uncertain fates. The lines of people were remarkably orderly. Jack sat behind the kid in the canoe and felt something in the pocket of his coat. He stuck his hand inside it and withdrew a folded pamphlet. *Midnight Sun*, it read in bold black letters.

Midnight sun? Jack knew this was the term given to the sun appearing very late at night in certain months of the year in places north of the Arctic Circle. He had a hard time reading the pamphlet's tiny, badly produced writing but it seemed a lot like religious propaganda to him.

Two burly men shoved the canoe, and Jack gripped the sides of the vessel as they shot forward. He should have been relieved, except he was terrified. He couldn't explain the feelings, the mounting terror he experienced. The long evening he and Sean had endured together came back to him.

He closed his eyes for a moment. He felt light-headed. How the hell had he wound up here? And why did the kid think this would lead them to safety?

Think, Jack, think.

What had the kid said? Aliens are afraid of water. That was true for the most part. Nicky had been terrified of bathing.

Jack began to yawn. Not a good sign. Lack of oxygen. How far north were they? Were they in high altitude?

He shook himself awake and tried desperately to focus on the pamphlet.

It stated that the world had been plunged into a new ice

age by scientists to control people's minds.

Whaaa? He read on.

Scientists have colluded with Aliens to take over our planet and enslave humans.

Aliens are afraid of water. The only way to travel is by water. Canoes leave every ten minutes. If you have received this flyer, then safety is only a short step away. No cash required. Midnight departure is the last voyage until six a.m. First come, first served basis only. Bring ONLY what you can carry.

He wanted to laugh out loud. This was ludicrous. *Wasn't it?* He tried to read on, but his eyes kept closing. The only sound was of somebody sobbing ahead. A woman, he thought. And the constant whack of the oars against the ice.

Rest. I need rest. And I need to think. God, I'm thirsty. I'm like that guy in the poem. Water, water everywhere, but not a drop to drink.

The canoe's movements, the sound of sobbing giving way to the oars moving, lulled him into sleep. Jack yawned and found as soon as he closed his eyes, Sean was waiting for him. Jack smiled. They were home. Back in Mexico. They should never have befriended anybody. They should have kept to themselves. The aliens would never have found them.

But we did keep to ourselves.

Oh . . . Sean. Oh, God. He is so beautiful.

"Is it really you?" he asked, stepping forward into the light and warmth of their bedroom. He reached out, and Sean grabbed his hand. "It's really me."

"You're naked."

"I was waiting for you."

"Huh." Jack ran his hands over Sean's hard body. He licked each bar of muscle on Sean's six-pack, paying special attention to his nipples and his belly button. He loved how

Sean jolted when Jack's tongue touched him there. Jack swiped long flat licks across his groin and around the base of his cock, finishing gently with little tugs on his foreskin with his lips.

"We need to finish this in bed." Jack swept Sean into his arms and into the bedroom, his cock still hard and hot against Jack's chest. Jack gave the tip a kiss, then took Sean's face in his hands, kissing him.

"I love the way you do that." Sean's voice grew husky. "Now put me on the air bed."

Air bed? When had they ever had an air bed?

"It's not very fancy. You deserve better, Jack."

Jack realized now that they were back in the bungalow in the Angeles National Forest where they'd hidden out before fleeing California.

"For fuck's sake shut up, get naked, and put your cock inside me," Sean griped.

Jack laughed. It was so unusual for Sean to beg to be fucked. Normally, a lot of bargaining was involved. "I'll get naked, but I am nowhere near ready to fuck you," he said.

Sean's gaze was intense, but Jack sensed his distraction. What was going on?

Heck. He's trying to tell me something.

Sean lay on the bed, watching Jack strip off his clothes in the increasingly bright sunlight. His smile was one of predatory pride when he saw how big Jack was. He kicked his feet with pleasure.

"Oh . . . Jack. I just *knew* you had a huge *monster* hidden in there. Please let me touch it." He sat up, his fingers running up and down the shaft. He placed a kiss on the head. Jack kept staring at him. *He's seen my cock before. What's he playing at?*

There was some hidden meaning in his words.

Jesus, Jack. Fucking think!

Aloud, Jack played the game. "Now that you two have

met, I've got a job to finish. Lie back, baby."

Sean smiled as Jack got between his legs, putting Sean's feet on his shoulders. Sean moaned as Jack went back to the job he loved more than anything, pleasuring his man with his mouth. He licked and sucked Sean's ass. Sean's hands flew to Jack's head. Jack didn't stop. He wouldn't stop. He ran his hand across Sean's belly, making him twitch at Jack's touch. Sean's feet came off Jack's shoulders, his knees lifted up, his legs opening up wide to Jack, who groaned, loving this new, closer access to him. He had to hold Sean tightly to him because Sean kept moving away from him in his bliss. Jack licked him for a long time until his tongue was numb.

Jack begged him over and over again to fuck him. Jack's cock was so hard he was afraid he would come before he was inside Sean.

He took his mouth off Sean, who pulled and grasped at him. Jack tore into him harder than he meant to, but Sean held him with his legs.

"Don't take it from me. Fuck me, Jack."

"I won't take it from you." *Why would he think that?* Jack worked his cock into him, drew back, then plunged into him again, and Sean held him even tighter. Those lovely legs took total possession of Jack as he came, red and gold fireworks blinding him, flooding his senses.

"Yes!" Sean screamed, and Jack had a feeling it had nothing to do with orgasms. Sean grabbed his own cock. He shouted Jack's name as he jerked himself to satisfaction, Jack reaching between their bodies to help.

Sean put his mouth to Jack's ear, his words coming out in a whisper.

"The water, Jack. Remember the fucking water!"

Jack's eyes flew open. *Holy fucking shitting shit.* He remembered now. Sean had prepared him for this, but Jack's treatment at the hands of the Greys had robbed him of his short-term memory.

"Attention everybody," he said. His voice was croaky.

Nobody seemed to hear him.

He began to yell to the other occupants in the canoe.

"It's all a lie!" he yelled, except that his voice came out a hoarse, crackly rasp. "It's all a lie," he said, forcing himself to say it louder.

"What's a lie?" the little kid in front of him asked, turning to look at him.

"The canoes aren't leading us to safety. It's a trick!"

"What are you talking about?" asked a man up front.

"What's he saying?" a woman asked.

"He says it's a trick," the man responded.

"It is a trick," Jack insisted. "Aliens are afraid of water, *cold* water. They thrive in warm water. These canoes are steering us straight into their comfort zone. They like warm water, particularly ballast water."

"Shut the fuck up!" people started yelling.

Jack stood. "We're heading straight into their trap!" he shouted, getting to his feet. The canoe shook, and people screamed.

"Sit down!" somebody shouted.

"Throw him overboard," another voice said. Jack repeated some of the things Sean had whispered to him in his small vision just now. He remembered a few things from their time together in Mexico. He had to get off the canoe. Had to get to Sean.

"Throw him!" the chant took up, and before he knew it, the little kid reached up and, with a super-human effort, tossed Jack overboard.

He plunged onto the ice, which gave way. A sickening crack and he began to sink into black water, the temperature of which almost killed him.

"If he gets back up, hit him in the head with an oar," he

heard a male voice say.

"What if he's right?" a small voice asked.

"He's not right. He's crazy!" another voice shot back. Jack looked up. The canoe was right above him. The ice was melting, the layers not so thick now. They were heading into . . .

Warmer waters. He hoped he could hold his breath long enough to get to the nearest patch of broken ice. He surged forward, holding his breath. The water turned paler and paler. A huge sea creature swam toward him, a gruesome, fierce-looking frilled shark.

The living fossil eyed him, its mouth open. As scary as the shark looked, its preferred choice of meal was plankton or octopus.

Jack dropped down, though his whole body screamed for air. He gently passed under the shark, estimating its eel-like body to be about twelve feet long. Its upper body turned around and swam straight for him.

He shot up again, taking his chances and opened his mouth to breathe.

Holy fucking hell.

He looked all around him. He couldn't believe what he was seeing.

Jack was in the middle of New York harbor, and all around him lay the bobbing, empty vessels of hundreds and hundreds of canoes.

Many of them dripped blood. Jack began to swim, but something grabbed his feet. Jack fought off the attack, looking down to see it was the frilled shark. Its bizarre teeth felt like sharp little needles, lots and lots of them sinking into his flesh. The pain made him cry out, but he grabbed onto a canoe and hoisted himself up, clutching a loose oar.

Jack hit the shark's flat snout, and it let go of him, a look of reproach in its creepy eyes. It wriggled away as Jack hauled himself into the rocking vessel.

He lay for several minutes, catching his breath. He sat up finally to check his bleeding ankles to find he was not alone. He stared at the end of the canoe, narrowing his eyes.

"What the . . ." he rasped, picking up the oar with trembling hands.

CHAPTER FOUR

Sean zeroed in on the canoe from the air and gasped as he recognized the figure who sat on the other side opposite Jack. These bastards would stop at nothing. He watched as Jack picked up the oar, then the man began to talk, leaning forward, extending his hand. When he did, Jack put down the oar. "No, no . . . fuck!" Sean muttered. He took out the detector and pressed the long-range function. He pointed it directly at the man in the canoe. It went red.

"That's not Dex. You know it. Dex is dead. Jack, please."

Sean knew he should do the same to Jack. He had to, but . . . if it went red . . . he took a gulp of air and shifted it over to Jack. *Green.* Oh thank God, they hadn't gotten to him yet. It wasn't too late.

Two hours ago he'd walked into a clandestine Air Force facility. He was looking for information, looking for a plane. As he walked down the silent halls, a voice said in his head: *Finally Sean. You're here. You're meant to be here. You know where to go.* And he did. He went underground, found the door, coded in the numbers . . . *666882. 666882. 666882.* The door opened, and there it was. He headed directly for the laptop, feeling like he was in some spy movie. He opened it. There was his commanding officer, a man he remembered as his friend and mentor. "James," he murmured.

Sean pressed the button.

"Captain Sean Delaney." The man saluted. "Only you could be listening to this right now. And I know you are. I knew you'd get here eventually. You're the best of us, man.

The information you were able to provide after your escape from abduction of Area 51 has been priceless."

"Escape from abduction," Sean mouthed.

"Now, listen carefully. What I'm about to tell you is current. This podcast is updated every six hours as necessary. In a box to your left, you will find all you need. We have developed a device allowing us to identify the aliens. You will quickly learn how to use it. Just point and click. Red means 'kill on contact.' In the hangar is a project we have worked on since the invasion. It is fashioned after a Boeing Stratofortress, long-range, subsonic, jet-powered strategic bomber."

"Say that ten times, boys and girls."

"You will be familiar with those, my friend. Remember the seventy-thousand pounds of weapons that baby can carry, Captain?"

"Yes, sir," Sean said to the screen. "I remember well."

"This one has sea capacity. It has four engines and can refuel at a touch of a button. It can reach the alien base in space and blow it to smithereens."

"My God."

"Captain, as of now, California and most of the other states are completely overrun with aliens. With the exception of Alaska, we have lost control of our country. We are now building a worldwide alliance, working closely with our nearest neighbors, the Canadians, who due to their colder climate, have fared far better. The news is, the colder the climate, the better. Also, there are some places so remote, they haven't discovered them yet. The divisions that existed politically between nations have broken down. We are all united against them. This is the only bright spot. All nations now have the technology to detect the aliens, thanks to the collaborative effort of scientists. I need you to fly that monster and come to us. I will disclose the location once you have her in the air. It is here you will join with us, and we will equip you for your mission."

Mission, Sean thought. He already knew what that was.

"That's all for now, Captain. You're a hero. Don't forget that. I hope to shake your hand soon."

The screen went blank.

Without delay, Sean opened the box. He found the device, more weapons, and a GPS system. He assumed this would lead him to where he needed to go.

Sean zoomed in on the scene below, magnifying everything on screen. It was amazing what this thing could do, and he hadn't discovered a quarter of it. People emerged from beneath the waves, bobbing up to the water's surface, staring up at him in terror as he pointed the device, setting it on long-range, and the thing went nuts, red, green . . . amber . . . shit. He had no way of knowing who was friend or foe unless he did each one. He couldn't take a chance. He only wanted Jack, but now Jack was clutching onto that thing's hand, something Jack thought was his husband. "Damn it, Jack." Sean picked up the mike and put it on loudspeaker. He had to get Jack away from that thing. "Jack! Listen, it's me! That's not Dex." Sean zoomed overhead and hovered there just above the canoe. People screamed and yelled, panicking as they grabbed for the canoes.

Where had they all been?

Jack glanced up at the Boeing, squinting in what suddenly seemed to be brutal sun. The canoe began to rock with the force of people trying to climb aboard. Damn it. Although in the sky where he was, it was cloudy. "Jack! I love you!"

Oh, man. He saw them then. Gigantic slug-like sea creatures slithering below, grabbing people who fought them off.

The other, detestable thing reached for Jack, turning itself into a hideous, scaly alien with razor-sharp claws. Jack was struggling with it. Damn it, Sean could have blown it into a thousand pieces, but he would kill Jack in the process. He had to land. He had no choice. He moved forward, scanning the land below, and then he saw them. They were everywhere, not even disguised. They were snatching up the unsuspecting passengers as they got to shore. This, he could do something about.

Sean released two bombs directly on the throng of aliens below. People screamed and scattered. Unfortunately, there was collateral damage, but that was unpreventable. He had destroyed a colony of the damn things.

"Whoa, baby!" he cried out. "I'm just getting started." He turned around and headed back over the water, scanning for Jack. Jack was in the water. Damn. Where in hell was that . . ."There you are . . ." Sean spotted the alien, and he was ready. "Jack," he called out on the mike, "swim away from the canoe and dive! Dive deep. Now!"

He watched Jack swim, then disappear under water. Sean dropped another bomb straight down. The canoe vanished along with the Dex look alike, pieces of it flying up into the air, causing Sean to abruptly raise his altitude to avoid being hit with it. He waited until Jack resurfaced, then turned around in the other direction. He headed to a strip of island far out in the choppy waves. He realized as he neared it that it was Mill Rock, a tiny island where the U.S. government once conducted atomic tests but was now a bird refuge. A few black herons swooped skyward as Sean, and the others approached. Sean hoped to hell Jack could swim that far and that it wasn't too cold. He'd just have to. There was no other way.

He had enough room to land, a few of the canoes pulling up to dry land. It wasn't going to be easy lifting off, however. Then he remembered, this wasn't just any jet. This damn thing had sea legs, and God knew what else, so they'd wing it. He settled, leaving the plane engines on. Sean jumped out of the pilot's seat and raced to the edge. He scanned the water. Jack was at least a mile out. Sean knew he was exhausted. He kicked off his boots and plunged into the water, his old navy rescue training still with him. He swam hard against the current. The water was icy cold, but he swam as hard as he could to warm his limbs. When he reached an exhausted Jack, he told him, "Float on your back. I'll pull you in."

Jack barely had enough strength to nod. Keeping a firm hold on him, Sean swam slowly back to the small island. When they were both on shore, breathing hard, Sean went to get Jack a blanket. He wrapped Jack in it and pulled him into his arms. He held him, trying to warm him up. It was some time before Jack could even speak. When he was warmer, Jack glanced at the fighter jet and grinned. "You like to make an entrance. I would have preferred a sports car though."

Sean chuckled. "Right. This is far better than any sports car, trust me." He got to his feet and pulled Jack up with him. "There are dry clothes in the jet. You need to get those wet clothes off. You all right?"

"I am now." Jack placed a hand over his eyes and scanned the other side. Smoke billowed up into the air.

"Come on, Jack. We have to leave here."

Jack followed him to the jet. "Where are we going?"

"We're going to one of the most remote and inaccessible places on Earth, Pitcairn Island in the South Pacific. It's where the Earth headquarters are located."

Jack blinked. "You mean where the *Bounty* was?"

Sean nodded.

"May I ask where you stole this baby?"

"Air Force base. And I don't think I stole it, technically. When I got to the base, there was a communiqué left for me on a laptop. I'll tell you everything once we're in the sky."

Jack glanced at him.

"Get in," Sean said.

After Jack had put on dry clothes and settled in the co-pilot's seat, Sean continued.

"Those in the know went to the South Pacific a while ago. The Air Force is conducting their operations there, along with some government officials from around the world. They were planning for this. They were waiting for me to remember."

"Remember what?"

"Remember all the information I gathered while I was in the hands of the aliens, Jack." He looked at him. "I think it was my mission to be captured."

"Oh, my God."

"I remember everything, all their plans, and their locations."

Jack looked terrified.

Sean reached for his hand. "It will be all right."

Jack swallowed hard and reached for Sean's hand. "Your mission; it's dangerous. You're going to war with them, aren't you?"

Sean nodded. He leaned over and kissed Jack. "I was one of the best fighter pilots they had. These new jets will allow us to penetrate their habitat beyond the stars."

"Like . . . Star Wars."

"Exactly. Ready?" Sean eyed him. "Buckle up. This thing moves."

"Sean?"

"Hmm?"

"How can you be sure I'm . . . you know?"

Sean leaned over and kissed him again. "I'd like to say it's in the kiss, but . . ." He laughed. "It's this." Sean reached into his pocket and pulled out a blinking device.

"What is it?" Jack asked, fascinated.

"A weapon developed by the military. It automatically

detects the aliens and allows us to destroy them when we point it straight at them." Sean pointed it at Jack and grinned. "You're not an alien, love."

Jack hugged his neck, then backed away. He sucked in some air. "Go!"

Sean nodded. He lifted up, pushing the water skis at the bottom forward and slid off into the water. He accelerated and, after going a few miles at mind-numbing speed, lifted smoothly into the air, pulling up the skis.

"Holy shit!" Jack called out. "Oh my God . . . it's like a fucking ride at Disney! And you really do know how to fly these things!"

Sean laughed. "Yep. I really do."

"It's sexy as hell."

"Oh?" He glanced at him with a grin. "Glad you think so. Hold that thought for later, okay?"

Jack reached over and squeezed his hand. "Will do. Oh, baby, I love you so much."

"I love you back."

"Are we going to have to set down to refuel?"

"No." Sean laughed. "It's wild. This thing refuels itself."

"Which way are we going?"

"Whichever way the course is set. I don't have control. It's done for me."

Jack chuckled. "I hear ya. Wow. Like a robot."

"Yeah, listen. Want to hear something neat?" Sean reached over and pressed a button.

A recording began.

"You are on course for the Pitcairn Islands, Captain Delaney, which is the official name for the Pitcairn, Henderson, Ducie, and Oeno Islands. These are a group of four volcanic islands in the southern Pacific Ocean that form a British Overseas Territory. The four islands – Pitcairn, Henderson, Ducie, and Oeno – are spread over several hundred miles of ocean and have a total land area of

about eighteen square miles. Only Pitcairn, the second largest and measuring about two and two-tenths miles from east to west, is inhabited. Current local population is forty-eight inhabitants. This population has swelled today to include military personnel and their families. Current total at this hour is seven hundred and forty-two.

The islands are inhabited by the descendants of the Bounty mutineers and the Tahitians — or Polynesians — who accompanied them. The history is still apparent in the surnames of many of the Islanders. With only about forty-eight inhabitants, currently from four main families — Christian, Warren, Young, and Brown — Pitcairn is the least populous jurisdiction in the world."

Sean switched it off.

"Wow. What else did it say?" Jack asked.

"Goes on to tell the history of the *Bounty* and such, also talks about the economy there, and how it has become a tourist destination."

"Really?"

"Um, yep."

"It's amazing the aliens didn't discover it."

"Too remote. There is an ocean mass of over one hundred miles between the islands, which for them, makes it inhabitable. "

"So Pitcairn is the only island there permanently inhabited."

"Pitcairn is accessible only by boat through Bounty Bay. Henderson Island covers about eighty-six percent of the territory's total land area, and supports a rich variety of animals in its nearly inaccessible interior. It is capable of supporting a small human population, but access is difficult, owing to its outer shores being steep limestone cliffs covered by sharp coral."

"How do you know all this stuff?"

Sean chuckled. "I listened to the intelligence bulletin on

the way to find you. It's really humid there, and the rainy season lasts from November to March, another reason the aliens wouldn't like it. The rain."

"Makes sense. And it's so fitting . . . the crew of *Bounty* mutinied and so shall we."

"You're so romantic." Sean leaned over quickly for a kiss.

"Hey, ah . . . if this thing can fly itself . . . Sean?"

Sean smiled. "What are you suggesting?"

"Well" — Jack reached over and placed a hand on his thigh — "I know we shouldn't but . . ."

It was true, Sean thought, and although he didn't want to say as much to Jack, they might not get another chance. He knew that as soon as he landed, after some much-needed rest, they'd be preparing him. Every moment that went by was critical.

Sean secured the jet on autopilot.

"How long do we have?" Jack asked him, squeezing Sean's thigh.

Sean checked the time. "Two hours."

"Well" — Jack unbuckled his seat belt — "let's not waste a second of it then."

Jack took him down on the floor, and he wasn't kidding about wasting time. Sean's body felt positively weightless as Jack pulled off his clothes and the jet glided at breakneck speed toward their destination. There was no turbulence or rough motion. All the action was coming from Jack, who had Sean's legs in the air and his pants off before Sean could say "hello there, how do you do!" Jack's hands roamed his chest, clawing at the buttons on Sean's shirt as he moved up between his open thighs and leaned in for a kiss. "Damn it, Captain, you're so damn hot."

Sean chuckled between kisses.

"You're . . . ah . . . um . . . pretty . . . um . . . um, . . . hot yourself there . . . co-pilot."

Jack lifted up and hastily stripped off his own clothes, tossing them here and there, then settled back on top of Sean. "Is that so?" he murmured, his mouth smothering Sean's again. "Well, you haven't seen anything yet, baby!"

Sean let his head go back as Jack trailed his lips down his throat and across his shoulder. He nibbled him there, then moved to Sean's left nipple, as Sean reached down to squeeze Jack's ass.

Jack wiggled closer, his erection brushing Sean's, and Sean made a pleasurable sound in his throat. Jack lifted his head and grinned, then licked down Sean's belly to his cock. He lifted Sean's legs up and began to lick and suckle Sean's cock, handling his balls with the other hand.

Sean grunted and lifted his hips off the floor.

Jack laughed and pressed him back down. "Easy there, soldier."

Sean licked his lips. "Okay, stop teasing me . . . oh . . . God . . ." Whatever Jack was doing down there, he didn't want it to stop. The guy had his cock in his mouth now, and it felt like he was swallowing it whole. "Um, do it . . . do . . . ooooh."

A hand reached under Sean's ass, and a finger stabbed into him. Jack went back to sucking him, then began to move his finger deeper.

"Stop . . . stop . . ." Sean pleaded. "I want to come . . . inside that gorgeous ass of yours . . . Damn, I'm going to . . ." It was too late. Sean's cock was ready, and he completely lost control of it.

Jack chuckled and rose to his knees. "Looks like your cock is out of control."

Sean nodded in agreement, then narrowed his eyes with a smile. "You will pay."

"Me?" Jack feigned innocence. "Can I help it if you have an unruly cock?"

Sean laughed and reached for Jack. He pulled him down into his arms, and they rolled around the floor of the jet. Sean tickled him, and Jack tried to get away. The constant interaction of their naked bodies was reviving Sean's cock, and it wasn't long until he was ready. "Okay," Sean announced, pinning Jack down under him, "my cock is ready."

"Um, is that so?" Jack looked defiant. "Well, maybe my ass isn't."

They were both breathing hard, both totally and completely turned on. Every inch of Sean's flesh was on hypersensitive alert. He let one of Jack's hands-free, and Jack reached up and ran his fingers over Sean's face and down his jaw. Even that was turning him on big time.

"You are so hot," Jack told him. "That shadow on your jaw, that face . . . so beautiful. Fuck." Jack raised his hips and rubbed his erection against Sean's thigh. Sean reared up between Jack's thighs, and Jack placed his hands on Sean's chest. He rubbed his palms over his pecs and nipples, causing them to noticeably stiffen. "Looks like you're erect everywhere," Jack murmured, then lifted up to lick his right nipple. "God, so beautiful, all of you." His tongue moved to the left one.

Sean tried to stay still as Jack ran his thumb over them now. "You feel that in your cock?"

Sean smiled. "Yeah, I feel it."

Jack pressed him back to the floor and began to kiss his chin, his chest, then he spread his legs and licked the length of Sean's cock. "So ready," he grunted.

"Yeah . . . I'm ready," Jack breathed.

Abruptly, Sean grabbed Jack's hips and flipped him onto his stomach, then he pulled him to his knees. "Not quite yet," Sean exclaimed. He pushed Jack's thighs wider and opened his cheeks. He began to slowly lick him as he played with Jack's cock and balls. He dipped his tongue inside him, tasting him, and continued to stroke his erection.

Sean could feel Jack trembling all over. He began to whimper, then to say, "Please."

"Please what?" Sean insisted, screwing his finger up inside of him.

"Oh . . . that . . ." He grunted. "Your cock . . . now."

Sean pressed the head of his cock into Jack's readied ass and pushed a little.

Jack cried out.

Sean pressed deeper, his hands on Jack's hips.

"Fuck me, baby . . . fuck the shit outta me!"

Sean let go and drilled in full tilt.

Jack let out a cry and reached back to cover Sean's hand with his own. Sean pressed Jack's head to the floor and nudged his thighs wider. He began to move in harder and faster, then slowed and moved side to side, lifting Jack's left leg so that he could go deeper still.

Their breathing came hard and fast, Jack crying out his name, and Sean closed his eyes, telling himself that if he wasn't successful, if he got captured and they took his mind . . . that he'd remember this . . . Jack crying out his name in pleasure. Laughing, sobbing . . . Sean ejaculated inside Jack, his hand coaxing Jack's cock to come with him.

Then they lay quiet, Sean on his back beside Jack, who had collapsed on his stomach. Jack turned his head and looked at Sean, a smile on his face. After a few seconds, he said, "Holy shit, baby, you really do know how to handle life equipment!"

Sean began to laugh. He reached over and pulled Jack's mouth to his. "I can't believe you said that."

Jack kissed him hotly. "How much time we got?"

Sean sat up and looked at the screen. "Another forty minutes."

Jack straddled Sean's hips. "Mercy," he drawled. "I'm dying for another ride on your rocket, Captain. Think you could accommodate?"

Sean could feel his cock begin to respond. "Think I'm about to refuel."

Jack moved down a little. "Let me help you, Captain. What kind of a co-pilot would I be if . . . well . . ." He licked his lips and studied Sean's reviving cock.

Sean reached over and pressed Jack's head to his cock. "Get to it then."

Jack sniggered before he began to stroke Sean's cock. It didn't take long for Sean to feel completely revitalized. He pulled Jack up and grinned at him. "My turn. Sit on my face, babe."

Jack met his gaze. "A man after my own heart."

"It's not your heart I want right now, stud."

Sean went to work again on Jack's ass, then pushed him down over his hips and winked at him. "Rocket is fueled, hot stuff. Take it for a ride."

Jack hovered over Sean's cock. With his hand he stroked it upwards several times. "Look at that baby stand at attention. Sean, you have a beautiful cock."

Sean reached out and stroked Jack's. "Yours is pretty special, and it belongs to me."

Jack nodded. "Oh yeah, no question of that, baby. Let's watch it disappear inside me, shall we."

Sean's head fell back as he felt Jack slowly swallow his cock with his ass. "Now" — Jack licked his lips and met Sean's eyes — "let me show you how your cock belongs to me. In fact, you belong to me completely, your cock, those delicious nipples, that ass . . . one I plan to take before we land this . . . oh God . . ." Jack moved down more on Sean's cock.

Sean held his breath.

"I plan to use your cock, then your ass. Can you take it,

Captain?"

Sean pushed up. Jack pushed back. "No. It's mine to use the way I want. Don't move."

"You're killing me here," Sean grunted.

"You want to thrust, don't you? Want to fuck the hell out of me?"

"Jack . . . please?" he pleaded.

Jack grinned, his hand playing with Jack's nipples. He pinched and tweaked them roughly for a few seconds, then moved a little on Sean's cock.

Sean moaned, his eyes closed.

"Don't come until I tell you to. I'm not ready," Jack told him.

"Move please," Sean pleaded. "Fuck me with your ass. Come on, baby."

Jack leaned in and kissed him, caressing Sean's nipples as he did, then he rose a little and came down on Sean's cock. They both moaned with pleasure. Jack did it again. They moaned again in unison, a little louder. Then Jack began to fuck Sean's cock in earnest, stroking his own cock as he rode Sean hard and fast. Sean shouted out his release, and Jack came off him. He lifted Sean's legs, dragged them roughly over his shoulders, and then thrust hard into Sean's ass. "So good . . . um . . . so damn good," Jack grunted.

Sean bit his bottom lip, tasting blood, as Jack continued to fuck him. Then he pulled out, pushed Sean onto his stomach and took him again. It was hard and rough and felt like pure heaven. Jack pulled him to his knees and handled his cock. "You're my slut, my whore . . . God, I love you so much. Sean! Jesus . . . ahhhhh!"

Sean felt Jack's come fill him and leak down his inner thigh, then Jack moved out of him. Sean closed his eyes. He almost went to sleep, then he heard Jack make a sound that sounded like a sob.

Sean turned around and sat up. Jack was sitting in the corner, his head down. "What is it? Jack, you okay?"

He glanced at him, his eyes red, tears on his face. "I'm so scared. Sean. I never thought I'd love someone the way I love you. What if . . . if I lose you?"

Sean quickly eliminated the distance between them. He held Jack close. "You won't. I promise."

CHAPTER FIVE

They could see the islands now. The screen in front of Sean flashed, and a voice-over said, "You are now approaching destination. A landing pad is located to your left. Please set course on number five on your control panel after you're contacted and clear your station command. Do you understand these directives, Captain Delaney?"

"Ten-four," Sean said. "Awaiting further instructions."

"Over and out, Captain. Good luck and have a nice day."

Jack's eyes widened. "Holy crap. Next, she'll be offering to suck you off."

Sean chuckled. "No, baby, that's your job."

"Nice work." He grinned. "Pay is crap, but . . . fringe benefits are out of this world."

Sean reached for Jack's hand. Below he could see a lot of activity. He set the course for five and hovered. "Come on," he murmured.

Suddenly another jet swooped up from out of nowhere and hovered a little way away. The radio crackled. "This is Air Force Command. Identify."

"Captain Sean Delaney. Good morning, Commander."

The radio came back. There was laughter. "You recognized my voice. How was the trip?"

Sean looked at Jack and grinned. "Very pleasant, indeed."

Jack winked at him.

"Good. Look, Sean, don't be alarmed but we must make sure you are really you. You got a passenger on board?"

"My partner. I used the device on him. He's okay."

"All right. We need to do the jet. Hold tight. It's going to feel like a force pulling at you, but it won't harm you. Take a breath, kids."

Sean's hand tightened on Jack's. They clenched their teeth as the plane was tested. They experienced a pressure, then a release.

The voice came back. "Welcome, Captain Delaney. You're set for landing. Follow me. Let's bring 'em in."

The next seventy-two hours went by so quickly, Sean hardly had time to breathe. He was told right away that he was the squadron leader for the U.S. team. Their target was the alien planet labeled Planet ET, for 'Enemy Target.' Given the fragility of the solar system, they couldn't just blast the planet. They'd have to land and fight the inhabitants on their home base.

"Hand to hand combat?" Jack was not happy. "Jesus, Sean, you don't even know what you're getting into. Can you even breathe the air?"

"We have equipment for that," Sean said. "Try not to worry."

"Worry? There are only a couple of safe places on this planet, closed-off havens in Canada's north, some forbidden frozen place in Russia, the mountains of Switzerland, and some places I've never heard of in China. What if there is no stopping these things?"

"They have weaknesses, babe." Sean hugged him. "We know what they are."

Jack sat in the corner, watching Sean suit up. Yes, he was terrified, and he was going to be stuck here waiting with the other families until Sean came back, *if* he came back. "Why can't I go with you?" Jack asked. "All able men should be—"

Sean walked over and placed a finger on his lips. "Because you're not a trained soldier and I am. Now, stop fretting. It's going to be all right. We have units from all over the world with us—Canadian, European, Asian, and . . . look, they can't kill us all."

Jack clung to him.

"I have to go."

Jack followed him out through the hallway of the newly built command center. Outside, a unit of his men waited, saluting as he walked past. Sean took one last look at Jack and waved, then got into the pilot seat of the jet. His co-pilot, a woman named Jean Freed, sat beside him.

"Ready?" he asked her.

"Ready, sir," she said.

The others filed on board and strapped themselves in behind them.

"Good luck, Captain." The Commander's voice came over the loudspeaker.

"Thank you, Sir," Sean said, eyes ahead. He said a silent prayer as he taxied the jet on the makeshift runway, the course set for space. *Take care, Jack, and may we be reunited one day soon.*

As it turned out, Jack wasn't to be idle on the island. Command put him to work in the intelligence center, receiving and transmitting information from around the globe and making sure the military stayed current.

Every hour, reports came in concerning the missing, and each missing person was automatically considered to have been taken by the aliens, stripped of everything that made them human.

When Jack had a break from the computers, he wandered along the hallways and read the information. At the end of the hallway, he stopped to see thousands of faces of people lost. They were in alphabetical order, name after name. He saw his parents, then he saw Dex. It was too much, and the tears rolled down his face. Dex had been taken at the same time Sean had come into his life. There, right next to Dex, was their son, Nicky. A woman came by suddenly and placed a hand on his shoulder.

Jack wiped his eyes and looked at her.

"You knew them."

He recognized her as a captain's wife, Audrey. "Yes" — he nodded — "my late husband and son. My parents, too. Damn."

"I'm so sorry," she said. "You're Sean's partner, aren't you?"

Jack smiled. "Yes."

"There's been so much loss. It never seems to end. You know, they picked up an orphan boy last night, a boy about the age of your son. He was just wandering around Death Valley."

"My God," Jack said. "Is he all right?"

"Yes. We don't know who he is. He's blocked out things. We can't get him to eat."

"Can I try?"

She smiled. "Sure. I'll bring you to him."

Jack followed Audrey down the hall to where the rooms were. She opened the door, and there sat a little boy around ten years old, dark hair, blue eyes . . . he could have been Sean's. He wasn't. This wasn't David, the half-alien, human spawn programmed to kill. This was a real little boy, lost, alone.

Jack approached slowly. "Hi. What's your name?"

The boy wiggled back on the bunk, fear in his eyes.

"I'm Jack. I'm a little lonely here. My partner is leading a mission right now, to space."

The small boy looked at him with some interest.

"Sean Delaney. You know who that is?"

He nodded.

Jack smiled. "Seems my partner is a hero already." Jack

swallowed and sat on a chair nearby. "I'm really scared. Could use someone to talk to."

"Why?" The boy asked. "Why are you scared?"

"I don't want to lose Sean. I'm afraid he won't come back."

"He will," the boy said softly.

"How do you know?"

He met Jack's gaze. "He's a hero. Heroes always come home."

Jack wanted to hug him so hard for that. "Thanks. So, I told you my name. What's yours?"

"Liam."

"Nice to meet you, Liam. You're safe here."

He shook his head. "No one is safe anywhere. They'll come for us soon."

Jack slowly moved closer. "I'll protect you if you'll let me. And when Sean comes back, he'll help me. He's pretty tough." As Jack spoke the words, tears formed in his eyes.

Liam got off the bed and walked over to Jack. "It's okay," he said. "He'll come back soon. And it will all be okay."

Jack couldn't help think what a remarkable boy he was, so battered by what had happened, and yet still compassionate enough to comfort Jack.

The days passed, and Liam stuck to Jack like glue. It didn't take long for them to bond. And as Jack continued to take in information, the havens around the world reported a significant decrease in attempted alien invasions of their territory.

It was working. The war was being waged in the stars, and it was working.

Every day Jack asked the top military officials for news on the war above. *Nothing.* They either had no way to communicate, or it was so classified that no one was privy to any information.

Jack took Liam around the island, and they watched and sometimes participated in the local economic activities. In spite of the fact that trade ships were temporarily banned, the locals still busied them with fruit growing and carving. Southeast of Adamstown, a lot of fruit was grown — including bananas, papaya, pineapples, mangoes, mandarins, watermelons, breadfruit, coconuts, avocados, and citrus. They also grew fresh vegetables like sweet potatoes, carrots, corn, tomatoes, taro, yams, peas, and beans. They harvested sugarcane, and a large variety of fresh fish was always available.

Liam was learning to carve from the locals who created sharks, whales, and turtles out of wood. They made models of the famous ship, *Bounty*, and weaved beautiful cloth.

Liam started to come alive again, be a little boy as he was meant to. And sometimes there were moments Liam made Jack truly happy and he almost forgot the war and the aliens. *Almost.* But when he lay in bed at night, Sean was not beside him. He was somewhere, millions of miles away, on some planet, fighting the most ruthless, ugliest, vicious species alive.

Sometimes Liam would crawl into bed beside him and sleep. If and when Sean came home, he'd ask him if they could keep Liam, adopt him. Jack just knew Liam and Sean would adore each other.

Months after Jack had first arrived on the tiny island, a loud siren blared in the middle of the night. Liam lay curled up beside Jack in bed, and he clung to him. "They're coming," he groaned.

Jack's heart beat hard in his chest. "Let's go," he said.

A voice sounded over the loudspeaker, asking everyone to meet in the assembly room. They all stood bleary-eyed and shivering, many in their bare feet, waiting. When the commanding officer took the microphone, his wife in her housecoat beside him, Jack clutched Liam's hand. "Please," he said aloud.

"Everyone," the commander said into the microphone, "I've just received a report from Captain Sean Delaney's crew. It's over! It's over. We've been liberated. The aliens have been destroyed!"

Jack began to sob as his boy hugged him. He picked Liam up and rushed to the front, pushing through the throng of excited people. "Commander?" he cried out. "Please, Sean . . . Captain Delaney, please . . . is he all right?"

The commander moved closer. He clamped a hand on Jack's shoulder. "He's coming home, son. Your man is coming home. And it's not Captain anymore; it's Commander."

Jack didn't give a damn if he was a private. He'd take him any way he could get him. "When?"

"They're on their way," the commander said. "They should get here some time tomorrow, our time." Someone pulled the commander away, and Jack gave Liam a kiss on the cheek. "I have a question for you."

Liam yawned. "What?"

"How would you like to be our son?"

"What if Sean doesn't . . . I mean, the captain . . . commander doesn't . . ."

"He'll love you just like I do, and you'll love him."

Liam grinned. "Everyone loves Sean Delaney now."

Jack carried the boy back to bed. "But he's mine." *And your dad, if it all works out.*

Jack couldn't sleep. He waited until Liam was sleeping, then went out to look at the stars. "Hey, baby," he said up at the night stars, "I sure can pick them. I never doubted you'd do this. I was afraid, but I should have known you'd come home to me. Hurry, honey. Please."

The following evening, Jack stood holding Liam's hand as everyone on the island waited. Ships sat on the water, film crews recording the heroes' homecoming. It was like that around the world. Since the news, the military had identified alien beings in every corner of the world, and they'd been destroyed. There was nothing about them that would allow for integration. They were a species bent on destruction. It was over, but those who had been taken weren't coming back.

When they heard the sounds of the jets scorching the skies, a cry rang out in the night. Fireworks went off, and several super jets scaled down to the landing pad. No one was allowed near the crew until they were on land. Jack had Liam in his arms so he wouldn't get trampled or lost. He waited, his heart bursting. Then Jack heard the applause, the cheers go up. *Sean.*

He came walking toward the crowd, one hand raised. He scanned the faces around him. Jack moved forward, but everyone wanted to be close to him, touch him. Jack wanted to touch him most of all.

Eventually, Jack gave up. He put Liam down and went back inside. "We'll wait. He'll come to us."

And he did. It was maybe twenty minutes later, the time it took Sean to move through the grateful crowd. He burst into the reception hall and stopped when he saw Jack. "There you are," he said.

Jack held the hand of a boy, a boy with dark hair and blue eyes. The boy pushed Jack forward, and Sean came to meet him. He enfolded Jack in his arms.

Jack reached out and touched Sean's face. "Hey you," he whispered. "God, I've missed you." He rubbed his rough jaw. "Sexy." Then he buried his face in Sean's shoulder and cried.

Sean's eyes blurred with tears as well. He hugged Jack

close, then kissed his lips tenderly. "I'm here."

Jack laughed and hugged him again. Then he separated himself and motioned to the boy. "Sean, this is Liam."

"Hello, Liam," Sean said, memories of his own son flashing in his mind. "How are you?"

"Will you be my dad, too?" he asked him.

Something stuck in Sean's throat. He looked at Jack and smiled, then looked down at the boy. "I guess I could manage that."

Liam threw himself against Sean, and Sean hoisted him up in his arms. He leaned his forehead against Jack's, then kissed it. He couldn't wait to make love to Jack.

Jack smiled, possibly reading his thoughts. "It's late," he said. "Let's say we put our son to bed, and, ah . . . you show me what a hero's bed looks like?"

Sean winked at Jack. "My pleasure."

Then Jack paused. "Oh damn, it's the people. There's a party in your honor and . . ."

"They've waited this long." Sean grinned. "Guess they can wait a bit longer . . . there are more pressing matters at hand."

Jack put an arm around Sean's waist and discreetly squeezed his buttock, as Liam dozed in Sean's arms.

Sean grinned, and they hurried off to their quarters.

You may also enjoy the following from eXtasy Books Inc:

Black Point
A.J. Llewellyn and D.J. Manly

Excerpt

"Can I come out now?"

"I thought you were out." Sandra Evans chuckled.

"Very funny," Thomas growled. "You know what I mean."

"You're a bestselling author, Tom. Why would you want to screw it all up?"

"Because I'm feeding a prejudice, helping to support the myth that men have no emotions."

"Don't be ridiculous. No one said men don't have any emotions. They said men can't write romance."

"Yes, apparently all men are capable of writing is porn."

His publisher laughed.

"It's not funny."

"Look, Thomas. Some people think that way, that's all. "

"That's why writers like me should reveal themselves."

"You into exhibitionism now? Hey, how about something like that in your next book? A male stripper who—"

"Sandra, focus. I'm dead serious about this. Why can't I

just come out and say my name is Thomas Carter?"

"Because your fans think you're Rose Carter."

"What in the hell difference does it make? My writing isn't going to change."

He could hear Sandra sigh on the other end of the phone. "Thomas, why this sudden interest in coming out as a man? Could it have something to do with Matt Malone?"

Matt Malone. Had it been that noticeable? "Well, he's out, he's a man and he's a writer in the same genre as I am. He even declared that he was gay the other night on my Yahoo group."

"My God, you've got a thing for Matt Malone!" She was howling with laughter.

"I do not."

"You're always flirting with him online. I've noticed that lately and he's flirting back."

"I do not flirt with Matt Malone. And Malone flirts with all the ladies. You're losing focus again, Sandra. My point is, he's a guy and he's accepted in this genre."

"Yes, but he only has two books out and you have over fifty. You started a few years back when all the writers were female, or at least, appeared to be. You're a top selling author, Thomas. A veteran. He's a virgin."

"I bet he's not a virgin," Thomas murmured.

"You know what I mean. We can't do anything to jeopardize your sales. I was talking to Matt the other day. He admires you."

"Yeah? What did he say about me?"

"He said, 'It's too bad Rose is female, she'd be perfect for me.'"

"That was low. He didn't say that."

Sandra was laughing again. "No, he didn't say that. It's a joke. He didn't say anything about you being a woman."

"Ahem, Sandra, I'm not a woman."

"I know that. He said you were his mentor. One of the reasons he had the courage to write was because of you. Not to mention that he jerks off to your books."

"I'm hanging up now."

She laughed again.

"Maybe we can just tell Matt I'm a guy?"

"We don't tell anyone. Matt could let it slip by accident. Now, get off this trip and get to work. I need those edits from you pronto."

"Yeah, yeah, you'll have the edits."

"And I expect you to be at the promo thing tonight. Your fans miss you."

"I'll be there. Haven't I shown up to most of them?"

"Except when you have some boyfriend problem."

"No worries. I'm temporarily boyfriendless, and you better hope I find a new one soon. My inspiration for those hot male-male sex scenes is quickly drying up."

"Try the personals. Hire a male hooker."

"You paying?"

"I will, if it means you'll give me three more books before the holidays."

"Classy."

"Hang up, Rose."

Thomas sighed.

"Oh, I have another idea—pick up one of Matt's books. You might find some inspiration there."

"I've read both of them."

"Pretty good, eh? You better go out to a gay bar, pick up some inspiration and then get your sweet ass back to the computer. And I've seen it. It's very, very nice."

"My computer?"

"No, your ass."

Thomas shook his head. "Good thing I love you."

"I love you, too, Rosie girl. Now write."

Thomas put down the phone.

Matt Malone was a brand new writer on the net. Sandra had accepted his first book two months ago. Since then, he had come out with a sequel, both complete with intriguing plots, gorgeous men and hotter than hot sex. Thomas had been intrigued by him almost immediately.

He was sociable, seemed anxious to get his name out there, and full of compliments for Thomas' writing. Experiencing a dry spell both in and out of bed, Thomas took the time to read Matt's work. He was impressed. His words jumped right out at him and held him captive, touching his very soul. It was as if Matt was speaking directly to him. Thomas took the time to drop him an email telling him how much he'd enjoyed the books. Matt wrote back almost immediately.

Rose,
My God, I'm speechless. Thanks so much. Coming from you, it means everything. I will keep this email for the rest of my life.
Matt

Thomas had no idea what Matt looked like, but he'd had some fantasies about that. He knew very little about him at all except that he lived at what seemed like the other end of the universe and he was gay. Somewhere he'd mentioned being in his early thirties, which was just perfect. He also mentioned that he didn't have a boyfriend, but that didn't make a hell of a lot of difference anyway since Matt thought he was some woman named Rose.

Thomas sat down at the computer and tried to write, but was distracted. He checked the clock. It was almost eight o'clock and their chat was at nine. He didn't have time to go out. Maybe later he'd hit the bars. It was Saturday night, after all.

Thomas got up and went to his closet. He took out a pair of black leather pants and a white silk shirt. He glanced at himself in the mirror. For a guy who had just turned thirty, he looked pretty damn good. Six foot two, slim and muscular, he put a lot of effort into staying in shape, especially since he spent so much time sitting in front of his computer.

His dark hair was layered back a bit and he'd finally got that shadow thing going on his jaw. Light blue eyes contrasted nicely with the thick chestnut colored hair. Men told him he was hot. He smiled at his reflection for a moment.

"Well, Matt, wonder what you would think if you could see Rosie now." He laughed at his little joke and shook his head. What in hell was this obsession he'd developed with Matt Malone anyway?

It made no sense. They weren't going to meet. And there wasn't even a possibility that Matt would ever imagine something happening between them because of his stupid masquerade. Oh well. He dumped the clothes on the bed and went back to his computer. He brought up Matt's latest book, Falcon's Fire. He scrolled down to the scene where one of the characters, a former next door neighbor who'd been enamored with the other guy for what seemed like eternity, finally get it on. And boy, do they get it on! Thomas smiled. He wondered if Matt worked from real life experiences like he did. If so, wow! Matt Malone would be one hot lover in bed.

Thomas snaked his hand down inside of his jeans and leaned back, reading the words out loud as he lightly stroked his cock.

ABOUT THE AUTHOR

A.J. Llewellyn lives in California, but dreams of living in Hawaii. Frequent trips to all the islands, bags of Kona coffee in her fridge and a healthy collection of Hawaiian records keep this writer refueled. A.J. loves male/male erotica, has a passion for all animals—especially the dog, the cat and the turtle. A.J. believes that love is a song best sung out loud.

To find out more about A. J., visit her at www.ajllewellyn.com, or you can email A.J. at AJ@AJLlewellyn.com.

D.J. Manly says, "I write not only for my own pleasure but for the pleasure of my readers. I can't remember a time in my life when I haven't written and told stories. When I'm not writing, I'm dreaming about writing, doing something wild and adventurous, or trying to make the world a better and more open-minded place to live in. I adore beautiful men, and I know I'm not alone in this! Eroticism between consenting adults, in all its many forms, is the icing on the cake of life!"

To find out more about D. J., visit the author's website at http://www.djmanlyfiction.com.

www.ingramcontent.com/pod-product-compliance
Lightning Source LLC
Chambersburg PA
CBHW070532130626
46555CB00003B/1389

* 9 781487 421779 *